Summer Weddings

A season of confetti and whirlwind romances!

You are cordially invited to attend the
Huntingdon-Cross summer weddings.

Celebrate the shotgun marriage of
Daisy Huntingdon-Cross and Sebastian Beresford
in

Expecting the Earl's Baby
by Jessica Gilmore

Save the date: on sale April 2015

Raise a glass to Rose Huntingdon-Cross and
Will Carter as they finally tie the knot
in

A Bride for the Runaway Groom
by Scarlet Wilson

Save the date: on sale May 2015

Join us in celebrating Violet Huntingdon-Cross
and Tom Buckley's star-studded wedding day
in

Falling for the Bridesmaid
by Sophie Pembroke

Save the date: on sale June 2015

FICTION

Dear Reader,

I love summer wedding stories and was delighted to be asked to be part of the summer wedding trilogy with Jessica Gilmore and Sophie Pembroke.

These three stories were plotted with a bottle of wine, sitting on some grass at the Romantic Novelists' Association conference in Newport, Shropshire.

I was so delighted when my hero, Will Carter, was nicknamed the Runaway Groom. As I was writing this story I could actually see a lot of these scenes in my head—particularly the one at the wedding fair when the balloons escape, and the final wedding scene in the tiny church on the island.

I love to hear from readers. You can find me at scarlet-wilson.com, on Facebook and on Twitter, @scarlet_wilson.

Enjoy!

Scarlet Wilson

A Bride for the Runaway Groom

Scarlet Wilson

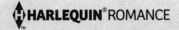

HARLEQUIN® ROMANCE

Recycling programs
for this product may
not exist in your area.

ISBN-13: 978-0-373-74337-7

A Bride for the Runaway Groom

First North American Publication 2015

Copyright © 2015 by Scarlet Wilson

HARLEQUIN®
™ www.Harlequin.com

Printed in U.S.A.

Scarlet Wilson writes romances and medical romances for Harlequin Mills & Boon. She lives on the west coast of Scotland with her fiancé and their two sons. She loves to hear from readers and can be reached via her website, scarlet-wilson.com.

Books by Scarlet Wilson

HARLEQUIN ROMANCE

English Girl in New York
The Heir of the Castle
The Prince She Never Forgot

Visit the Author Profile page
at Harlequin.com for more titles.

For two gorgeous brides who are now two fabulous mummies, Carissa Hyndman and Hayley Dickson.

And to my fellow authors Jessica Gilmore and Sophie Pembroke for making this such fun!

CHAPTER ONE

SOMETHING WASN'T RIGHT.

No, scratch that. Something was very, very wrong.

Everything should be perfect. Her sister's wedding yesterday had been beautiful. A picture-perfect day with a bride and groom that truly loved each other. It was a joy to be a part of a day like that.

But, by midnight, the days of jet lag that she'd been ignoring had finally caught up with her and she'd staggered to bed and collapsed in a heap, catching up on some much-needed sleep.

Her new brother-in-law, Seb, had a house to die for. Hawksley Castle, a home part Norman, part Tudor and part Georgian. The room she was in was sumptuous and spacious with the most comfortable bed in the world.

At least it would be—if she were in that bed alone.

She could hear breathing, heavy breathing,

sometimes accompanied with a tiny noise resembling a snore.

Right now, she was afraid to move.

She hadn't drunk much at all yesterday—only two glasses of wine. Because of the jet lag they'd hit hard. But not so hard she'd invited someone into her bed.

She'd attended her sister's wedding alone. No plus-one for Rose.

There had been no flirtations, no alluring glances and no invitations back to her room. And this definitely was *her* room. She opened her eyes just a little to check.

Yes, there was her bright blue suitcase in the corner of the room. Thank goodness. She hadn't been so tired that she'd stumbled into the wrong room. Seb's house was so big it might have happened.

But it hadn't.

So, who was heavy breathing in her bed?

She didn't want to move. Didn't want to alert the intruder to the fact that she was awake. She could feel the dip in the bed at her back. Turning around and coming face-to-face with a perfect stranger wasn't in her plans.

She needed to think about this carefully.

She edged her leg towards the side of the bed. Stealth mode. Then, cringed. No satin negligee. No pyjamas. Just the underwear she'd had on under her bridesmaid dress that was lying in a crumpled heap at the bottom of the bed. Brilliant. Just brilliant.

Her painted toenails mocked her. As did her obligatory fake tan. Vulnerable. That was how she felt. And Rose Huntingdon-Cross didn't take kindly to anyone who made her feel like that.

Just then the stranger moved. A hand slid over her skin around her hip and settled on her stomach. She stifled a yelp as her breath caught in her throat. Something resembling a comfortable moan came from behind her as the stranger decided to cuddle in closer. The sensation of an unidentified warm body next to hers was more than she could take.

She slid her legs and body as silently as possible out of the bed. The only thing close to hand that could resemble a weapon was a large pink vase. Her heart was thudding against her chest. How dared someone creep into bed with her and grope her?

She held her breath as her feet came into contact with the soft carpet and she automatically grasped the vase in both hands.

She spun around to face the intruder. In other circumstances, this would be comical. But, right now, it felt anything but comical. She was practically naked and a strange man had crept into bed beside her. How dared he?

Who on earth was he? She didn't recognise him at all. But the wedding of an earl and a celebrity couple's daughter was full of people she couldn't even take a guess at. Undoubtedly he was some hanger-on.

If her rational head were in place she would grab her clothes and run from the room, getting someone to come and help with the intruder.

But Rose hated being thought of as a shrinking violet. For once, she wanted to sort things for herself.

She padded around to the other side of the bed in her bare feet, hoisting the vase above her head just as the stranger gave a little contented moan.

It was all she needed to give her a burst of unforgiving adrenaline. The initial fear rapidly turned to anger and she brought the vase down without a second thought. 'Who do you think you are? What are you doing in my bed? How dare you touch me?' she screamed.

The vase shattered into a million pieces. The guy's eyes shot open and in one movement he was on his feet—fists raised and swaying.

He blinked for a few seconds—big, bright blue eyes with a darker rim that didn't look the least bit predatory, but a whole lot shell-shocked—then dropped his fists and clutched his head.

'Violet, what on earth are you doing? Are you crazy?' He groaned and swayed again, one of his hands reaching out to grab the wall—leaving a bloodstained mark on the expensive wallpaper.

She couldn't breathe. Her heart was thudding against her chest and her stomach was doing crazy flip-flops. 'What do you mean, *Violet*? I'm not Violet.'

This just wasn't possible. Okay, Violet was her identical twin. They didn't usually look so similar, but a few years stateside and not seeing each other on a daily basis meant she'd shown up with an identical hairstyle to her sister.

This clown actually thought he was in bed with her sister? What kind of a fool did that?

He was still shaking his head. It was almost as if his vision hadn't quite come into focus. 'But of course you're Violet,' he said.

'No. I'm not. And stop dripping blood on the carpet!'

They both stared down at the probably priceless carpet that had two large blood drips, and the remnants of the vase at his feet and across the bed.

He grabbed his shirt from the chair next to the bed and pressed it to his head. It was the first time she'd even noticed his clothes—discarded in the same manner as her yellow and white bridesmaid dress.

His eyes seemed to come into focus and he stepped forward, reaching one hand out to her shoulder. He squinted. 'Darn it. You're not Violet, are you? You haven't got her mole on your shoulder.'

His finger came into contact with her skin and she jumped back. One part of her knew that this 'intruder' wasn't any danger to her. But another part of her was still mad about being mistaken for her twin and being felt up by her twin's boyfriend. How on earth could this be explained? This guy was obviously another one of Violet's losers.

Violet burst through the door. 'What's going on? Rose, are you okay?' Her eyes darted from one to the other. The guy, in his wrinkled boxer shorts and shirt pressed to his forehead, and Rose, in her bridesmaid underwear. The broken vase seemed to completely pass her by.

She wrinkled her nose in disgust and shook her head. 'Will? My sister? Oh, tell me you didn't?'

They didn't sound like words of jealousy—just words of pure exasperation.

She threw her hands in the air and spun around, muttering under her breath. 'Runaway groom my sister and I'll kill you.'

Rose was feeling decidedly exposed. The only thing she could find to hold in front of herself was her crumpled bridesmaid dress.

Whoever he was, he obviously wasn't Violet's boyfriend—not with that kind of reaction. But did that make things better or worse? She'd still been groped by an absolute stranger.

He wobbled again and sagged down into the chair strewn with his clothes, arching one eyebrow at her. 'So, crazy twin. Do you assault every man you meet?'

'Only every man who climbs into my bed uninvited and cops a feel!'

'Well, lucky them.' He sounded oh, so unimpressed. Then he frowned. 'Did I touch you? I'm sorry. I was sleeping. I didn't even realise I'd done that.'

The blood was starting to soak through his shirt. She cringed. Maybe the vase had been a bit over the top. And at least she'd got some kind of apology.

She stepped forward and took the shirt from his hand. 'Here, let me.' She pressed down firmly on his forehead.

'Youch! Take it easy.'

She shook her head. 'The forehead's a very vascular area. It bleeds easily and needs a bit of pressure to get the bleeding to stop.'

'How on earth would you know that?'

'Friends with children who seem to bang their foreheads against every piece of furniture I own.'

He gave her half a smile. It was the first time she really noticed how handsome he was. There were no flabby abs here. Just a whole load of nicely defined muscles. With those killer blue eyes and thick dark hair he was probably quite a hit with the ladies.

A prickle flooded over her skin. In the cold light of day this guy seemed vaguely familiar.

'How do you know Violet?' she asked.

He winced as she pressed a little harder. 'She's my best friend.'

Rose sucked in a deep breath. Things were starting to fall into place for her. Because she'd been working in New York she hadn't met Violet's best friend for the last few years. But she had heard a lot about him.

She pulled her hand back from his forehead. Now she understood what Violet had said. '*You're* the Runaway Groom?' She was so shocked she dropped her dress.

A single dark red drop of blood snaked down his forehead as he looked at her in disgust.

'I hate that nickname.'

The Runaway Groom. No wonder he looked vaguely familiar. He'd been on the front page of just about every newspaper in the world. Self-made millionaire Will Carter had been famously engaged three—or was it four?—times. He'd even made it down the aisle once before turning on his heel and bolting.

The press should hate him. But they didn't. They loved him and ate it up every time he fell in love and got engaged again. Because Will was handsome. Will was charming. And Will was sitting semi-naked in front of her.

She was trying so hard not to look at the abs and the scattering of dark hair that seemed to lead the eye in one direction.

She gave herself a mental shake just as a heavy drop of blood slid past his eye and down the side of his face. She leaned over to catch it with the shirt, just as he lifted his hand to try and brush it away.

The contact of their skin sent a tingle straight up her arm, making her heart rate do a strange pitter-patter. All the little hairs on her arms stood on end and she automatically sucked in her stomach.

'Look, I'm sorry about your head. But I woke up and there was a strange man in bed with me— then you touched me and I was frightened.' And she hated saying those words out loud but since she'd caused bodily harm to her sister's best friend it seemed warranted. She raised her eyebrows. 'You're lucky it was only a vase.'

His gaze was still on her. 'So you're Rose?' It wasn't really a question—more an observation and it was obvious from his expression that a million thoughts were currently spinning through his brain. What on earth had Violet told him about her?

He looked at the fragments beneath his feet and gave a half-smile. A cute little dimple appeared in one cheek. 'Oh, you're definitely not going to be Seb's favourite sister-in-law. At a rough guess that's over two hundred years old.'

A sick feeling passed over her. Defence was her automatic position. 'Who puts a two-hundred-year-old vase in a guest bedroom? He must be out of his mind.'

He shrugged. 'Your sister obviously doesn't think so. She just married him.'

Daisy, Rose's youngest sister, was still floating happily along on cloud two hundred and nine. And Seb seemed a really sweet guy. Just as well since she'd told her sisters just before the wedding that two were about to become three. The first baby in the family for more than twenty years. Rose couldn't wait to meet her niece or nephew, and she was doing her best to ignore the vaguest flicker of jealousy she'd felt when Daisy had told her.

She frowned. How much did a two-hundred-year-old vase cost anyway? She lifted the shirt again and winced. 'Hmm.'

His eyebrows shot up. 'What's "hmm"?'

'*Hmm* means it's deeper than it originally looked and I think you might need stitches. Maybe I can get you a packet of frozen peas from the kitchen?' She paused and looked around. 'Do

you even know where the kitchen is in here?'
Even as she said the words she almost laughed
out loud. Seb's kitchen would probably spontaneously combust if someone even said the words
'frozen peas' in it. Daisy really had moved into
a whole different world here.

He shook his head and placed his hand over
hers. His hand was nice and warm, whereas hers
was cold and clammy. Another thing to annoy
her. He wasn't nearly as worked up as she was.
This was all just another day in the life of the
Runaway Groom. How often did he wake up next
to a strange woman?

'What were you playing at anyway? You might
be Violet's best friend but why on earth would
you be climbing into bed with my sister? It's obvious from Violet's reaction that there's nothing
going on between you. What on earth were you
doing?'

Will gestured his head towards her suitcase.
'If I'm going to need stitches why don't you get
dressed? You'll need to take me to the hospital.'

He hadn't answered her question. Did he think
she hadn't noticed? Of course she had.

And the assumption that she'd take him to the
hospital made her skin bristle.

All of a sudden she was conscious of her dis-
tinct lack of clothes. She slid her hand out from
under his and moved over to her suitcase, curs-

ing herself when she remembered he'd just had a big view of her backside.

Still, if he sometimes bunked in with Violet, then he was used to being around her sister in a semi-naked state. She glanced backwards. He didn't seem to have even noticed. Was she relieved or mad? She couldn't work it out. Apart from a few freckles, moles and little scars—one of which he'd already noted—she and her sister were virtually identical. Maybe that was why he wasn't looking? He'd seen it all before.

She grabbed a summer dress from her case and pulled it over her head. A little rumpled and yesterday's underwear still in place. Not the best scenario. But she didn't fancy fishing through her smalls to find a new set while he sat and watched in his jersey boxer shorts that left nothing to the imagination.

'Don't you have a bride in waiting that can take you to hospital?'

He scowled at her. 'Not even funny, Rose. You work in PR, don't you? Surely you know better than to believe everything you read in the papers?'

His words were dripping with sarcasm. The nerve she'd apparently just touched ran deep.

She folded her arms across her chest. 'But I thought most of the time you sold those stories and worked them in your favour.'

'What made you think that?' he snapped.

'Oh, I don't know. The ten-page photo spreads in *Exclusive* magazine. How many of them have you featured in now?'

He gritted his teeth together. '*Not* my idea.'

It was good to see him uncomfortable. Waking up with a strange guy in your bed was horribly intimidating. To say nothing of the discomfort and embarrassment. What if she snored—or made strange noises in her sleep?

And he still hadn't answered the question about sleeping with her sister. What exactly was the deal? His eyes were still fixed furiously on her and the blood was soaking through his shirt. She decided to give him a little leeway.

She gestured towards him. 'What about you? You can't wear that shirt. Where are your clothes?'

He wrinkled his nose. 'I'm not sure. I ran in here at the last minute yesterday. I think my bag might be in Violet's room.'

'Violet's room?' She said it bluntly, hoping he'd take the hint and decide he should go there. But if he did, he ignored it.

'Yeah, would you mind running along and grabbing something for me?' He had that smile on his face. The one that was usually plastered all over the front page of a magazine, or on his face when he was charming some reporter. It was almost as if someone had flicked a little switch and he'd just fallen into his default position. His voice and smile washed over her like a warm summer's day. Boy, this guy was good. But she was determined not to fall for his charms.

'I will. But only because I've probably scarred you for life. I'm not Violet. I'm not your best friend—or your bed buddy. Once I've taken you to the hospital, we're done. Are we clear?'

His Mediterranean-sea-blue eyes lost all their warmth. 'Crystal.' He waited until she'd reached the door before he added, 'And you're right. You're not Violet.'

He watched her retreating back as she stomped out of the door. His head was definitely muggy and he wasn't quite sure if it was from the alcohol last night or the head injury this morning.

Part of him felt guilty, part of him felt enraged and part of him was cringing.

Last night was a bit of a blur. He'd just made it to the wedding on time and hadn't eaten a thing beforehand. His charity commitments were hectic and he was anxious not to let people down, which meant he'd been pulling on his tie and jacket in the sprawling car park at Hawksley Castle. A business call had come in just as dinner had arrived so he'd missed most of that, too. Then the party had truly started. And Violet had mentioned something about staying in her room as she'd fluttered past in her yellow and white bridesmaid dress.

A bridesmaid dress he'd definitely seen on the floor as he'd stumbled into the room. She'd been sleeping peacefully with her back to him and he hadn't even thought to wake her. Actually, he knew better. If he'd shaken Violet awake to let her know he was there she would have killed him with her bare hands.

Maybe the sisters had more in common than he thought?

It was strange. He'd never once considered Violet in a romantic sense. They'd clicked as friends from the start. Good friends. Nothing more. Nothing less.

He trusted her. Which was a lot more than he could say of some people. She gave it to him straight. There was no flirting, nothing ambiguous. Just plenty of laughs, plenty of support and plenty of ear bashing.

But Violet's identical twin… Well, she was a whole different story.

It didn't matter they looked so similar it was scary. They were two totally different people. No wonder they got annoyed when people mixed them up. And you couldn't get much more of a blunder than the one he'd just made.

But it wasn't the blunder that was fixating in

his head. It was that little missing mole on her left shoulder. The memory of her skin beneath the palm of his hand. And the site of her tanned skin and rounded backside when she'd turned to get dressed. They seemed to have imprinted on his brain. Every time he squeezed his eyes shut, that was the picture he saw inside his head.

He stood up and walked over to the en suite bathroom. He grimaced when he saw his face. It was hardly a spectacular sight. His shirt—worn once—was ruined. Not that he couldn't afford to buy another one. But he'd picked this one up especially for the wedding. Even millionaires didn't like waste.

He stuck his head back out of the bathroom door. Maybe he should put his trousers back on? Meeting someone for the first time dressed only in jersey boxers was a bit much—even for him. But every time he lifted his hand from his forehead the blood started gushing again. Struggling into a crumpled pair of trousers one-handed was more than he could think about.

He couldn't help but smile. He knew Violet well. Her sister Rose? He didn't know her at all. This was their first meeting. And she obviously wasn't bowled over by him.

Will wasn't used to that. Women normally loved him. And he normally loved women. This was a whole new experience for him.

There was more to Rose Huntingdon-Cross than met the eye. And he'd already seen more than his fair share.

He could even forgive the Runaway Groom comments. Violet said her sister was a PR genius and she'd handled the whole publicity for their father's upcoming tour and charity concert.

Maybe he should get to know Rose a little better?

Rose strode down the hall. She could feel the fury building in her chest. The audacity of the guy. Who did he think he was?

She pushed open the door of her sister's room. 'Violet? What on earth is going on? Why would the Runaway Groom be in bed with me—and think I was you? Why would you be in bed with that guy? And why would there be touching?'

Violet was leaning back on her bed drinking tea, eating chocolate and reading a celebrity magazine. She lifted her eyebrows at her sister and started laughing. 'You didn't hook up with Will?'

'No! I didn't hook up with Will! I woke up and he was lying next to me. He thought I was you!'

Violet folded her arms across her chest and looked highly amused. 'He doesn't like the Runaway Groom tag.'

Rose rolled her eyes. 'So I gathered.'

Violet grinned. 'Will copped a feel?'

Rose shivered and waved her hand. 'Don't even bring that up.'

Violet shrugged and continued to drink her tea. 'So, it was a simple mistake. I'd say send him back along the corridor, but...' she paused and raised her eyebrows, giving Rose that oh, so knowing smile '...I'm thinking this looks a whole lot more interesting than that.'

'What's that supposed to mean?' Rose was getting mad now. Neither Violet nor Will was really giving anything away about their relationship and she couldn't understand why it irked her so much.

'Violet, come and take your plaything back. I don't have time for this. I've got a hundred things to sort out for Dad's tour. Another set of wedding rings to make for a couple who are getting married in two weeks. And a runaway groom who needs his head stitched. Be a good sister and take him to the hospital for me?'

Violet shook her head and jumped off the bed. 'Not a chance, dear sister. You caused the injury. You can try and make it up to Will. He can be very good company, I'll have you know.'

She gave Rose a little nod of approval. 'By the way, Daisy and Seb's wedding rings? Probably the nicest I've ever seen. That's what you should be doing. You're wasting your talent running Dad's tours for him.'

Rose sighed and sat down on the edge of the

bed. A little surge of pride rushed through her chest. Violet's opinion mattered to her. 'Making those rings was the best thing I've ever done, Vi. I know I've made lots of different pieces for people before. But making something for your sister?' She smiled and gave her head a little shake. 'And watching the person she loves with her whole heart give it to her and knowing that she'll wear it for a lifetime? You just can't beat that.'

A flicker of something passed over Violet's face. Not annoyance. Not frustration. Just... something.

'I'll make your wedding jewellery for you, too,' she added quickly.

Violet let out a laugh. 'I'll need to find a groom first. In fact, we both do. Our baby sister's gone and beat us to it.'

Rose leaned backwards on the bed, propping herself up with her elbows. 'I know.' She lifted one hand up. 'And she's done it in such style. Do we really need to call her Lady Holgate now, or Countess? Because I can tell you right now—' she shook her head '—it's never, *ever* going to happen.'

The two of them laughed out loud and collapsed back onto the bed. 'Daisy Waisy it stays.'

Rose turned her head to look at her sister, leaning over and picking up a strand of her blonde hair. 'You know, Vi, we almost look like twins,' she said sarcastically. 'We'll have to do something about these hairdos.'

Violet sighed. 'I know. I couldn't believe it when I saw you the other day. Maybe I'll go back to curls.'

'Don't you dare. That frizzy perm was the worst thing I've ever seen.'

Violet laughed and shook her head. 'Oh, no, the worst thing *I've* ever seen was you kissing Cal Ellerslie at that party years ago.'

Rose's shoulders started shaking with laughter and she shuddered. 'Oh, yuck, don't remind me. I still feel sick at the thought of that. He was all tongue. The guy had no idea what he was doing.'

She turned on her side and rested her head on her hand. 'Is there anyone you've been kissing lately?'

Violet sighed again. 'You're joking. There are absolutely no decent men around.'

'What about Will—your runaway groom?' She was prying and she knew it. But she couldn't help but ask the question out loud. Violet had been talking about Will for months. Maybe Rose just hadn't been paying enough attention.

But Violet's eyes widened. 'Are you joking—Will?' She let out a snort. 'No way. I mean, I love him to bits—just not like that. Never like that. I trust Will. Completely. I've been in his company lots of times, sometimes even raging drunk. He's a gentleman through and through. He's the kind of guy that sees you home, puts you to bed and stays with you until morning.' She wrinkled her nose. 'In fact, I've done the same for him. We're good company for each other.' She smiled. 'And every time he gets engaged, I get to buy a new wedding outfit with matching shoes and bag. What more could a girl want? Even if they never get an airing.'

Rose rolled her eyes. She knew better than most that Violet couldn't care less about wedding outfits, shoes and handbags. She was much more down-to-earth than most celebrities. They all were. 'Yeah, right.'

But Violet had drifted off. Her eyes were fixed on the ornately decorated ceiling, carved with cherubs. 'There's just no spark between us, Posey. None. Not even a little zing, a little tingle.' She turned her head to face her sister on the bed. 'You know what I mean?'

Oh, boy, did she. She'd felt that little tingle shoot up her arm like an electric shock. She blinked. Her sister was looking at her with her identical big blue eyes. They were unyielding. Their bond was strong. She'd always been able to see inside Rose's head—even when Rose didn't want her to.

Rose shifted uncomfortably on the bed. But

Violet blinked. For once, she was lost in her own little world. 'I mean, there's got to be someone out there.' She regained her focus. 'For both of us,' she added quickly.

Rose smiled. It was the first time she'd ever seen her sister actually contemplate a future partner. Maybe the fact their younger sister, Daisy, had beat them both up the aisle and was going to be a mother had made their biological clocks start to tick. It was an interesting concept. And one she wasn't quite sure she was ready to explore.

Coming back to England had been hard enough. Visiting in the last three years had been painful. Everything seemed to be a reminder of that dreadful night a few years ago. The one that was imprinted on her brain like a painful branding.

But sisters were sisters. She couldn't really stay away too long. She still spoke to, Skyped or emailed her sisters every day. Not even an ocean—or a tragic death—could come between them.

But now her father's tour was coming back to Britain. It was big news for the band. A re-launch after a few quiet years—with only an annual charity concert—followed by a brand-new album. And she had to be here, in England, to deal with the last few PR issues. Her quietly building wedding jewellery business would have to be pushed to the side for a few months. She needed time to focus on the final details of the tour.

The last thing she needed was any distractions. And that was exactly what the Runaway Groom was—a distraction. Even if he did make her arm tingle.

Rose rolled off the bed. She hated that little feeling at the pit of her stomach. The one that had given a little flutter when her sister had assured her there was nothing between her and Will.

Nothing at all. Funny how those words were so strangely satisfying.

CHAPTER TWO

THE FROZEN PEAS were a godsend. It appeared that Hawksley Castle did have some—even though Rose had doubted. The lump on his head wasn't quite so big and, as long as he kept them pressed to his head, the bleeding stopped.

He'd managed to struggle into the T-shirt and jeans that Rose had brought from his bag in Violet's room. But instead of leaving him alone to get dressed, she'd leaned against the wall with her arms folded.

'What, no privacy?'

'From the guy who was in my bed? You lost the privacy privilege a while ago, mister. Anyway, hurry up. I've got things to do today.'

'Really? I would have thought after your sister's wedding you might want to chill out a bit.'

She crossed the room as he slid his feet into his training shoes. 'I'd like to have time to chill out, but I don't. I've got the final touches to make to my dad's tour, then I need to finish some jewellery for another bride.'

He looked up. 'Ready. Do you know where the nearest hospital is?'

She nodded. 'I know this area well. Let's go.'

They walked down the corridor and out of the front doors of Hawksley Castle. She opened the door of a pale blue Rolls-Royce and nodded at him to get in the other side.

Will couldn't hide the smile on his face as he slid into the cream leather seat. 'Didn't take you for this kind of car,' he said in amusement.

She started the engine and frowned at him. 'What kind of car did you think I'd drive?'

'Something sporty. Something small. Probably something red.' He looked thoughtful for a second. 'Probably one of those new-style Minis.' He wasn't revealing that his identical Rolls-Royce was parked a few cars down in the car park.

She pulled out of the car park and down the sweeping mile-long driveway. 'This is my dad's. You forget, I've been in New York for the last three years. There isn't much point in me having a car here right now, so I just borrow one when I'm home.'

'And he lets you?' Rick Cross's car collection was legendary. 'How many does he actually have?'

She laughed. And it was the first genuine laugh he'd heard from her. It was beautiful. Light and frivolous. Two things that Rose didn't really emanate. 'You mean, how many does Mum think he has—or how many does he *actually* have?'

Now Will started laughing. 'Really? How does he manage that? Where on earth can he hide cars from her?'

She shrugged. 'He's a master. We've got more than one home. You'll have seen the garages at Huntingdon Hall. There are eighteen cars there. Four in New York. Three in Mustique. And—' she glanced over her shoulder as if to check if someone was there '—another twelve at an unspecified location in London.'

'Another twelve? You've got to be joking.'

'I never joke about my father.' She shrugged. 'What can I say? It's his money. He can spend it how he likes. Same with my mother. They have beautiful homes, there might even have been the odd nip and tuck here and there, and to the outside world they seem like a pretty frivolous couple.'

He could hear the edge in her voice. Just as he'd heard the same tone in Violet's voice on a few occasions. He'd met Rick and Sherry. They seemed like regular, nice folks. Polite, well-mannered, and they obviously loved their daughters.

'So, what's the problem?'

Her head whipped around. 'Who said there was a problem?'

'You did. Just now.'

'I did not.'

He sighed. 'You and Violet are more alike than you think. She does that, too—starts talking about your parents and then starts to say strange things.'

'She does?' Her voice was a little squeaky and her knuckles turned white on the steering wheel. It was nothing to do with her driving. And nothing to do with the car.

The Rolls-Royce was eating up the country roads with ease. It should be a pleasant enough drive. But Rose looked tense.

'You must deal with the press all the time. Why does it annoy you when they describe your parents as frivolous?'

'Because they're not really. Not at heart. Yes, they spend money. But they also give a lot away. Lots of celebrities do. My mum and dad both support lots of charities.'

He nodded. 'Yeah, I remember. I've seen her in the magazines and doing TV interviews.'

'That's what you see. What you don't see is all the work they don't let the public know about. My dad does a lot of work for one of the Alzheimer's charities. He doesn't tell anyone about it. My mum works on a helpline for children. She sometimes does a twelve-hour shift and then goes out to do her other charity work.'

'That sounds great. So, why are you annoyed?' He couldn't understand why either of the sisters would be unhappy about their mum and dad doing good work.

'Because they are so insistent that no one finds out. Sometimes I think they're working themselves into the ground. To the world they seem quite frivolous. But they're not like that in person.'

'I don't get it. Why the big secret? What's the big deal?' His arm was beginning to ache from holding it against his head. He might be a millionaire himself, but even he didn't want to risk bleeding all over the inside of Rick's precious car.

Rose turned the car onto a main road, following signs toward the hospital. 'Because they don't want people to know. My uncle—my dad's brother—has Alzheimer's. He developed it really early. It's in my dad's family and he says it's private. He doesn't want people knowing that part of his life and invading my uncle's privacy. Mum's the same. She says the calls from the kids are all confidential. If people knew she worked there, the phone line would probably get a whole host of crank calls that would jam the lines.'

He nodded. 'I get it. Then, the kids that needed to, couldn't get through.'

She pulled into the hospital car park. 'Exactly.'

'So, your parents do something good.' He waited while she pulled into a parking space. 'I can relate to that.'

'You can?' She seemed surprised.

'Yeah. I do a lot of work for one of the homeless charities. But it doesn't get a lot of good publicity. It's something I need to think about.' He gave her a smile. 'Maybe you could give me some advice? You do PR for your father? Maybe you could tell me what I should be doing to raise the profile of the charity.'

She gave the slightest shake of her head. 'Sorry, Will, but this is it for me. I've got a hundred and one things to do in the next few weeks. I don't even know how long I'll be staying. Once your head is stitched I need to get back to work.'

He climbed out of the car, still pressing the now unfrozen peas to his head. Rose was intriguing him. He could use someone to give him PR advice. Someone who knew how to try and spin the press. Maybe he should try and persuade her?

The woman behind the desk didn't even blink when he appeared at the desk. 'Name?'

'Will Carter.'

She lifted her eyebrows and gave a half-smile. 'Oh, it's you. Did one of those brides finally give you the smack you deserved?'

He couldn't help but smile. 'No. I'm all out

of brides at the moment—have been for a little while.' He glanced towards Rose, who was looking distinctly uncomfortable. 'It was just a friend who did this.'

A nurse walked towards them and the receptionist handed her a card. 'Will Carter, the Runaway Groom. Head injury.' She rolled her eyes. 'What a surprise.'

The nurse gave a little grin and nodded her head. 'This way.'

'Come on.' He followed the nurse down the corridor and gestured to Rose to follow them.

Her footsteps faltered. It was obvious she didn't really want to come along. But Will had just been hit by a brainwave. And a perfect way to make it work.

'I'll just sit in the waiting room,' she said quickly. She'd no wish to see Will Carter getting his head stitched. Even the thought of it made her feel a bit queasy.

'No, you won't.' His voice was smooth as silk. 'I want you with me.'

The nurse's eyebrows rose just a little as she pulled back the cubicle curtains. 'Climb up on the trolley, Mr Carter, and I'll go and get some supplies to clean your wound.'

She disappeared for a second while Rose stood

shifting self-consciously on her feet, not quite sure where to put herself.

'What's wrong, Rose? Don't like hospitals?'

'What? No, I don't mind them. I just would have preferred to sit in the waiting room.'

He lifted the peas from his head. 'Don't you want to see the damage you've done?'

Her face paled. 'But I didn't mean to. I mean, you know that. And what did you expect? You climbed into bed with a perfect stranger.'

The nurse cleared her throat loudly as she wheeled the dressing trolley into the cubicle.

Rose felt the colour flood into her cheeks. Twenty-seven years old and she was feeling around five. 'I didn't mean... I mean, nothing happened...' She was stumbling over her words, her brain so full of embarrassment that she couldn't make sense to herself, let alone to anyone else.

The nurse waved her hand as she walked to the sink and started scrubbing her hands. 'Everything's confidential here. My lips are sealed.'

'But there's nothing to—'

Will was laughing. He leaned over and grabbed her hand. 'Leave it, Rose. You're just making things worse.' As he relaxed back against the trolley, his hand tugged her a little closer. There was a gleam of amusement in his eyes. Mr Charming wasn't flustered at all and it irked her.

'I kind of like seeing you like this.' Even his voice sounded amused. She'd never wanted out of somewhere so badly. She could practically hear the waiting room calling her name.

'Seeing me like what?' she snapped. The nurse had finished washing her hands and was opening a sterile pack and some equipment on the dressing trolley. She couldn't wipe the smile from her face.

Will's dimple appeared. 'You know—babbling. Violet doesn't get like this at all. It's quite nice to see you flapping around.'

'I'm not flapping around. This is all your fault anyway—and you know it.'

The nurse lifted the peas from Will's head and deposited them in the bin. 'Youch,' she said, pulling a head lamp a little closer. 'It looks as though you might have a tiny fragment in your wound. What caused your injury?'

'She did.'

'A vase.'

Their voices came out in unison. Rose was horrified. He'd just told the nurse this was her fault. The nurse's eyes flickered from one to the other. Thank goodness she was bound by confidentiality, otherwise this would appear all over the national press.

But she was the ultimate professional. She picked up some swabs and dipped them in the solution on the dressing trolley, along with a pair of tweezers. 'Brace yourself, Mr Carter. This is going to sting a bit. I'm going to give this a clean, then try and pry out the little piece of vase that is embedded in your wound. Five or six stitches should close this up fine.'

'Five or six?' Rose was beginning to feel light-headed. 'Can't you just use that glue stuff?'

The nurse shook her head. 'Not for this kind of wound. It's very deep. Stitches will give the best result—and hopefully the least amount of scarring.' She pulled up some liquid into a syringe. 'I'm just going to give you an injection to numb the area before we start.' Her experience showed. The injection was finished in a few seconds. 'It will tingle for a bit,' she warned. Her gaze shot from one to the other. 'I'm obliged to ask, but I take it from your tone this was an accidental injury?'

Rose felt her cheeks flame. 'Absolutely.' She couldn't get the words out quickly enough.

Will was watching Rose with those dark blue-rimmed eyes. She saw a flicker of something behind his eyes. He looked at the nurse with a remarkable amount of sincerity. 'Rose wouldn't normally hurt a fly. There's nothing to worry about. So, you said I'll definitely have a scar, then?'

'Yes.' She nodded as she cleaned the wound.

'Think of yourself as Harry Potter.' She gave a little laugh. 'I hear he gets all the girls.'

Was it hot in here? Or had she just forgotten to put deodorant on this morning? It was getting uncomfortably warm. She pulled her dress away from her body for a few seconds to let the air circulate.

Will was still watching her as he continued his conversation with the nurse. 'Will it be a bad scar?'

Rose shifted on her feet. Boy, he was laying it on thick. Stop talking about the scar. Guilt was flooding through her. She'd just scarred a man for life. And it seemed as if he'd talk about it for ever.

The nurse bent forward with her tweezers, then pulled back. 'Here it is!' She dropped the microscopic piece of vase on the dressing trolley. How on earth had she even seen it?

She gave Will's head a final clean, then picked up the stitching kit. 'This won't take long. I'll give you some instructions for the next few days.' She glanced towards Rose. 'When the vase hit you—were you knocked out?'

'No,' he said quickly. 'I was sleeping and, believe me, once the vase hit I was wide awake.'

Rose rolled her eyes and looked away. He was making a meal of this. It was clear the nurse was lapping up his Mr Charming act. And it was making her more than a little uncomfortable.

Because, like it or not, it was hard not to get pulled in. One look from those big eyes, along with the killer smile and dimple, was enough to make the average woman's knees turn to mush.

No wonder this guy got so much good press. Why on earth would he think he needed any help?

She fixed her eyes on the floor as the nurse started expertly stitching the wound. Will Carter, Runaway Groom would now have a scar above his left eyebrow. A scar that *she'd* caused. It was definitely making her feel a bit sick.

The stitches were over in a matter of minutes and then the nurse handed Will a set of head injury instructions. 'You shouldn't be on your own for the next twenty-four hours.' She gave Rose a smile. 'I'm assuming that won't be a problem?'

'What? You mean me? No. No, I can't. Will? I'm sure there must be someone who can keep you company for the next twenty-four hours.' A wave of panic was coming over her.

But Will shook his head, then lifted his hand towards his head. 'Ouch.'

The nurse moved forward again and looked back to Rose. 'This is why he really needs someone to be around him. There can be after-effects with a head injury. If you can't supervise he'll need to be admitted to hospital. Are you sure you can't help?'

Her tone was serious. It was obvious she was apportioning the blame at Rose's door. The words were stuck in her throat. And as the guilt swamped her she couldn't think of a single good reason to say no.

Will leaned forward a little. The tiniest movement. The nurse had her back to him with her hand on her hip. Will's face appeared through the gap at her elbow and he pointed to his head. 'Scarred for life,' he mouthed before giving her a wink.

The cheeky ratbag. He was trying to blackmail her. And she hated to admit it—but it was working.

'Fine.' She snatched the instructions from the nurse's hand. 'Anything else?'

The nurse switched on her automatic smile. 'Not at all.' She turned to Will. 'Pleasure to meet you, Mr Carter. Pay special attention to the instructions and—' she glanced at Rose '—I wish you well for the future.' She wheeled her dressing trolley out of the cubicle.

Rose was fuming. Half of her thought this was all his own fault, and half of her was wondering if the millionaire would sue her for personal damages. She'd heard of these things before. What if Will couldn't sell his next wedding to *Exclusive* magazine because of his scar?

What if he sold the story of how he got his scar

instead? She groaned and leaned back against the wall.

'Rose, are you going to pass out? Sorry, I didn't think you were squeamish.'

She opened her eyes to face his broad chest. He'd made a miraculous recovery and was standing in front of her with his hand on her arm to steady her.

The irony wasn't lost on her. *She* was supposed to be looking after *him*—not the other way about.

He'd told her he needed help with publicity. Maybe she'd unwittingly played into his hands? Her brain started to spin.

Her head sagged back and hit against the cold hospital wall. Her eyes sprang back open and he was staring right at her again.

How many women had he charmed with those blue eyes? And that killer dimple…

His arm slid around her shoulders. 'It's hot in here. Maybe you'll feel better if we get some fresh air.'

His body seemed to automatically steer hers along. Her feet walking in concordance with his, along the hospital corridor and back out to the car park. Her first reaction was to shake off his unwanted arm.

But something weird was happening. Her body seemed to enjoy being next to his. She seemed to fit well under his shoulder. In her simple sundress the touch of his arm across her shoulders was sending little currents to places that had been dormant for a while.

Twenty-four hours. That was how long she would have to be in his company.

Panic was starting to flood through her, pushing aside all the other confusing thoughts. This guy could charm the birds from the trees. She'd thought she'd be immune. But her body impulses were telling her differently.

As soon as the fresh air hit she wriggled free from under his arm. 'I'm fine.' She walked across the car park and jiggled her keys in her hand.

'We need to have some ground rules.'

He leaned against the Rolls-Royce. She could almost hear her father scream in her ear.

'What exactly might they be?' One eyebrow was raised. He probably couldn't raise the other. That part of his forehead would still be anaesthetised. Darn it. The guilty feelings were sneaking their way back in.

'I think when we get back to Hawksley Castle we should ask Violet to stay with you. After all, she knows you best. She'll know if you do anything out of character—like grope strange women.' She couldn't help but throw it in there. She waved the instructions at him. 'You know, anything that might mean you need to go back to hospital.' Now she was saying the words out loud they made perfect sense.

He waved his finger at her. 'Oh, no, you don't.'

'Don't what?'

'Try and get out of this.' He pointed to his forehead. 'You did this to me, Rose. It's your job to hang around to make sure I'm okay.'

He was so smooth. A mixture of treacle and syrup.

'Oh, stop it, Will. I'm not your typical girl. I'm not going to fall at your feet and expect a ring. And if you keep going the way you are I'll hit you again with the next vase I find. I've got things to do. I can't hang around Hawksley Castle.'

He smiled and opened the car door. 'Who said we were spending the next twenty-four hours at Hawksley Castle?'

She started as he climbed in. She pulled open the car door and slid in. 'What on earth do you mean? Of course we're going back to Hawksley Castle.'

He shook his head. 'I think both of us have overstayed our welcome. You've damaged one of Seb's precious heirlooms and I've probably put immovable stains on an ancient carpet and wall. I suggest we regroup and go somewhere else.'

She started the engine. 'Like where?'

'Like Gideon Hall.'

Gideon Hall. Will Carter's millionaire mansion. At least at Hawksley Castle she'd be surrounded by family and friends. There was safety in numbers. Being alone with Will Carter wasn't something she wanted to risk.

'Oh, no. I need to work, Will.'

'I can give you access to a phone and computer. What else do you need?'

'My jewellery equipment, my soldering iron, my casting machine. My yellow, white and rose gold. My precious stones. Do you have any of those at Gideon Hall?'

The confident grin fell from his face. 'You're serious about making the jewellery?'

His question annoyed her. 'Of course I am. Working for my dad is the day job. Working to make wedding jewellery? That's the job I actually want to do. I spend most of my nights working on jewellery for upcoming weddings. I have an order to make wedding rings for a bride and groom. I can't afford to take any time off.'

It was nice to see his unwavering confidence start to fail. It seemed Mr Charming hadn't thought of everything.

She sighed. 'If need be, we can collect our things from Seb's, then go back to my parents' place. If you've hung around with Violet long enough you must be familiar with it.'

He settled back in the chair. 'Do you have your equipment at your parents' house?'

She nodded. 'I have one set in New York, and one set here.'

'That's fine. We can move it to my house in the next hour. I'll get someone to help us.'

He pulled his phone from his pocket and started dialling. 'What? No. What on earth is wrong with you? I've said I'll hang around you for the next twenty-four hours. Isn't that enough?'

He turned to face her. 'Actually, no, it's not. I've got a meeting later on today with a potential investor for the homeless charity. It's taken for ever to set up and I don't want to miss it.'

'Can't you just change the venue?'

Will let out a long, slow puff of air and named a footballer her father had had a spat with a few months ago. 'How would your dad feel about him being in his house?'

She gulped. 'Wow. No. He'd probably blow a gasket. He hates the guy.' She frowned. 'Are you sure he's the right kind of guy to help your charity?' She was racking her brains. Her dad was a good judge of character. He could spot a fake at twenty paces and didn't hesitate to tell them. She was sure there was a good reason he didn't like this footballer—she just couldn't remember what it was.

Will still couldn't frown properly. It was kind of cute. 'I've no idea. I've never met him before. But he's well known and popular with sports fans. It's not so much about the money. It's the publicity I need help with. We need to get the homeless agenda on people's radars. They need to understand the reason people end up on the streets. It's not just because they're drunks, or drug addicts or can't hold down a job.'

She turned back into the grounds of Hawksley Castle. 'You're really serious about this, aren't you?'

'Of course I am. Why would you think I'm not?'

She bit her lip. 'What's in it for you? Why is a homeless charity your thing?'

It took him a few seconds to answer. 'I had a friend at university who ended up on the streets. I didn't know. He didn't ask anyone for help because he didn't want anyone to know the kind of trouble he was in. I found out later when someone tried to rob him and stabbed him in the process. The police found my details amongst his things.'

She pulled the car to a halt and turned to face him. 'Was he dead?'

Will shook his head. It was the first time she'd really seen complete sincerity on his face. No charm, no dimple, no killer smile. In a way, it made him all the more handsome even though she tried to push that thought from her brain.

'No. But Arral needed help. And there's a lot more people out there who need help, too.'

'So, you really want good PR to raise awareness and you think this footballer will give you it?'

He folded his arms across his chest. 'Is that scepticism I hear in your voice, Rose?'

She gave him a smile as she opened the door and took the key from the ignition. 'I just don't know if he's your best choice.'

Will climbed out next to her. 'Neither do I, but, right now, he's my only option. How long will it take you to grab your stuff?'

She shrugged. 'My clothes? Five minutes. What about my equipment?'

'I'll arrange for someone to go your parents' and pick it up. Do you want to drop by first?'

She nodded. 'It won't take long. Let me get my clothes and I'll meet you back here.'

Will was true to his word. There was a man with a van waiting outside her parents' house when they arrived. She took him around to her workshop and collected the things she'd need to start work later that night.

As she was collecting a few other items her father appeared. 'Oh, hi, Dad. I didn't expect you to be back yet. I thought you'd still be at Hawksley Castle.'

He smiled. 'Your mother and I came back an hour ago. We had a few things we wanted to discuss.'

Her mother appeared at her father's side, his arm slipping around her waist and resting on her hip. Sherry Huntingdon still had her model-girl looks and figure even though she was in her fifties.

Rose's father's face was a little more lived-in. Rock and roll did that to you. His hair was still longer than normal—he still loved the shaggy rock-star look.

Rose's stomach started to do little flip-flops. Her father's words were a bit ominous. He had a tendency to spring things on her. And it looked as if nothing was about to change.

Rick crossed the room and put his hand out towards Will. 'Will, aren't you hanging around with the wrong daughter?' There was an amused tone in his voice. 'And what happened to your head? Did one of those brides finally get you?' He threw back his head and let out a hearty laugh.

Rose cringed. How many times was Will going to hear those words?

But Will seemed unperturbed. 'Ask Rose—she was the one that socked me with a vase.'

'She what?' Rose's mother seemed shocked.

Rose waved her hand quickly. 'It was a misunderstanding. That's all. What did you come back to talk about, Dad?' She wanted to distract them before they asked too many questions.

Her mother and father turned and smiled at

each other. There it was. That sappy look that they got sometimes. In a way it was nice. Still romantic. It was obvious to the world that they still loved each other.

It was just a tad embarrassing when it was your parents.

'Your mother and I have made a decision.'

'What kind of decision?' She had a bad feeling about this.

Both of them couldn't stop smiling and it was making her toes curl. She just knew this was going to be something big.

'After all the preparations for Daisy's wedding—and the fact everything went so beautifully—your mother and I have decided to renew our wedding vows.'

'You have?' It was so not what she expected to hear.

Her mother put her hand on her father's chest. She was in that far-off place she went to when ideas started to float around her head. 'You know we never had a big wedding.' She turned to acknowledge Will. 'We ran away to Vegas and got married after only knowing each other for a weekend. I never really had the fancy dress, flowers or meal like Daisy had. So, we've decided to do it all again.'

Rick shrugged and smiled at Will. 'It might

seem hasty, but believe me—' he smiled at his wife '—when you know, you just know.'

A thousand little centipedes had started to crawl over Rose's skin. She had a horrid feeling she knew exactly where this was going.

'It's a lovely idea. When were you thinking? Next year—after the tour is over?'

'Oh, no.' Rose's mother laughed. 'In a few weeks.'

'A few weeks!' She couldn't help but raise her voice. Will shot her a look, obviously trying to calm her. But he had no idea what was coming next. Rose did.

Sherry stepped forward. 'What's the problem? We have the perfect venue.' She spun around. 'Here. We just need a marquee for the grounds. And a caterer. And some flowers. And some dresses.' She turned to Rick and laughed. 'And a band!'

Rick stepped forward. 'It shouldn't be a problem. You can arrange all that in a few weeks, can't you, Rose? You do everything so perfectly. And you're just so organised. We couldn't possibly trust anyone else with something so important.' Her father stepped over and gave her a hug and dropped a kiss on her cheek. It was clear he was floating on the same love-swept cloud that her mother was.

'Me?' Her voice came out in a squeak as Will's eyes widened in shock.

Oh, now he understood. This was what she got for doing such a good job. She was the official PA for her father's band and her mother's career. With all the tour preparations she barely had time to sleep right now. But she loved her parents dearly so she let them think it was all effortless. Her parents had been so strong and so supportive when she'd needed them—even though she secretly felt she'd disappointed them. Their love and support was the only thing that had got her through. All she wanted to do was make them proud. If they were trusting her with something like this? It made her anxious to please them, to let them be confident in her choices, even if this was the last thing she needed.

Her father's voice was steady. 'You know just how hard your mother's been working recently. And what with planning Daisy's wedding, she's just exhausted. If you could do all this it would be a whole weight off our minds.'

The dopey smiles on her parents' faces were enough to melt her heart—even though it was fluttering frantically in her chest and her brain was going into overdrive.

Will seemed to pick up on her overwhelming sense of panic. He stepped forward. 'What a fantastic idea. But these things normally take a while to plan—don't you want to wait a while and get everything just right?'

It was a valiant attempt. But Rose knew exactly how this would go. Once her parents got an idea in their heads there was no changing their minds.

Rick gave a wave of his hand. 'Nonsense. It didn't take long to sort out Daisy's wedding, did it?' He gave Rose *that* look. The one he always did when she knew he meant business. Rick Cross had invented the word *determined*.

'I'm not sure, Dad. There's a lot to do, what with the tour and the charity concert and everything.'

His hand rested on her arm and he glanced in his wife's direction. 'Now, Rose. Let's give your mother the wedding she always deserved.'

The truth was he wasn't picking up her cues. He was too busy concentrating on the rapt expression on his wife's face. Anxiety was building in her stomach. If she could do this, maybe she could repay her parents for everything they'd done for her. When she'd been splashed over the press when her friend had died she couldn't have asked for better advocates or supporters. Family was everything.

She started to murmur out loud. 'But I know nothing about weddings. Receptions, marquees, dinners, dresses…'

Her mother smiled. 'Oh, honey. Leave the dress to me. I'm going to get the one I always wanted.' Her gaze locked with Rick's and it was clear they were lost in their own little world.

Rick waved his hand. 'Ask Daisy. She knows all about it.' He let out a little laugh. 'Or ask your friend. He's had his fair share of organising weddings.'

Her parents turned and drifted back out of the room, lost in conversation with each other. That was it. Decision made. And *everything* left to Rose.

Rose turned to face Will. Her tongue was stuck to the roof of her mouth. She'd kill for a cosmopolitan right now. Her mouth was so dry she couldn't even begin to form words. She'd been blindsided. By her parents.

Will was looking just as pale.

She lifted her hands. 'I... I...' But the words wouldn't come out. The only sound that did come out was a sob. All this work. Organising a wedding in a few weeks might be okay for some people. But some people weren't Rick Cross and Sherry Huntingdon. They'd have a spectacular guest list—who'd all come with their list of demands. Where on earth would she find the kind of caterer she'd need at short notice? Her parents were very picky about food.

And what was worse—already she wanted it to be perfect for them.

Her heart was thudding in her chest. The more she thought, the more she panicked. Her chest was tight. The air couldn't get in. It couldn't circulate. Tears sprang to her eyes.

Will stepped straight in front of her. 'Rose? Sit down. You're a terrible colour.' He pulled a chair over and pushed her down onto it, kneeling beside her. 'In fact, no. Put your head between your legs.'

The inside of his palm connected with the back of her head and pushed down. She didn't even have time to object.

The thudding started to slow. She wasn't quite so panicky. After a few seconds she finally managed to pull in a breath.

This was a nightmare. A big nightmare. She didn't have enough hours in the day to do what her parents wanted. But how on earth could she say no?

She lifted her head a little and a tear snaked down her cheek. She wiped it away quickly.

Will looked worried. 'There must be someone else who can organise this for them? What about your sisters? They can help? Or can't you hire someone?'

'To organise my own parents' renewal of vows? How, exactly, would that look?' She waved her hand. 'And Daisy might just have done it all but she's off on her honeymoon to Italy for the next two weeks. Violet knows as much about weddings as I do.' Her voice cracked as their gazes collided.

And something in her head went *ping*.

'Will, you have to help me.'

A furrow creased his brow. The anaesthetic had finally started to wear off. 'But isn't it supposed to be the other way? I wanted you to give me some advice about PR for my homeless charity.'

She straightened her shoulders and drew in a deep breath. Things were starting to clear in her head. She wasn't dumb. Only an hour ago Will Carter hadn't been above trying to blackmail her. Head injury or not—it was time for her to use the same tactics.

'Dad was right. You have the perfect skill set to help me out here. Help *us* out.'

Realisation started to dawn on him and he shook his head. 'Oh, no. Your dad wasn't being serious.' It was his turn to start to look panicked.

She smiled. This was starting to feel good. 'Oh, I think he was.'

She placed her hands on her hips as she stood up. Will was still kneeling by her chair. It was the first time she'd been head and shoulders above him. There was something empowering about this. She held out her hand towards him. This might be the only way out of this mess.

'Will Carter? If you want my help, then I want yours.' She could feel herself start to gain momentum.

'You can't be serious.'

'Oh, but I am. I help you and you help me.'

He stood up. 'Do what exactly?'

There was something good about the way he mirrored the same panicked expression she'd had a few minutes earlier.

She stretched her hand a little further. 'I help you with your PR. You help me with this crazy wedding renewal.'

He shook his head. 'I think you've got this all wrong. I only ever made it to one wedding. The rest never got anything like that far. Sure, I helped with some of the planning but that doesn't make me an expert. The label in the press—Runaway Groom—it doesn't really mean that. I've never even been a groom.' He was blustering, trying anything to get out of this. 'I don't even like weddings!' was his last try.

She pressed her lips together to stop herself from laughing out loud. She liked seeing him floundering around. Will Carter liked to be in control. Liked to be charming. She could almost feel the weight lift from her shoulders. This might even be the tiniest bit fun.

She smiled at him. 'Will Carter? I think you're about to be my new best friend.'

The Runaway Groom was starting to look a whole lot more interesting.

CHAPTER THREE

WILL WAS STARTING to freak.

What had started as a bit of flirting and curiosity was turning into something closely related to the things he normally fled from.

It didn't matter that this was someone else's wedding. Weddings were the *last* thing he wanted to get involved in.

Except, he'd said that before. Four times exactly.

And he always meant it. Right up until he met the next girl—the next love of his life—and things went spectacularly. The romance, the love, the inevitable engagement, the press and then the plans started.

Everything always started swimmingly. Beautiful, fairy-tale venues. Wonderful menus. Great bands.

Then, things started to get uncomfortable. Fights about meaningless crap. Colours, ties or cravats, kilts or suits. Sisters and mothers-in-law interfering in he didn't even know what.

Arguments about wedding vows, dresses—spectacular scenes about dresses having to be ordered eighteen months in advance and not arriving in time. Ridiculous costs for 'favours'—things that no one even cared about and everyone left lying on the dinner tables anyway.

Tantrums over cakes. Tantrums over cars.

And love dying somewhere along the process. But it wasn't the wedding process that really did it for him. It was that feeling of *for ever*. That idea of being with one person for the rest of your life. Whenever his bride-to-be had started talking about wedding vows Will always felt an overwhelming sense of panic. And all of a sudden he wasn't so sure.

It didn't help that he knew his friend Arral's wife had walked out and left Arral when he'd lost his job. It had all contributed to Arral sinking into depression and ending up homeless. For better or worse. Someone to grow old with. The theory was great. But what if when the chips were down his potential bride-to-be decided she didn't want for ever any more?

He didn't really understand why, but as the wedding date drew nearer Will always had a massive case of cold feet. Actually, it wasn't cold feet. More like being encompassed by the iceberg that had sunk the *Titanic*.

The trouble with being a nice guy was that

it was hard to realise when exactly to back out. Once, he'd got right to the main event, but had backed out in spectacular fashion, earning him the nickname the Runaway Groom.

Even now he winced and closed his eyes. His bride-to-be had sensed his doubts and made veiled threats about what she might do if he didn't turn up.

So, he'd turned up. And made sure when he left she was surrounded by family and friends— even if all the family and friends were about to do him a permanent injury.

Violet had a theory on all this. She said that he hadn't met the right girl yet. Once he had? Everything would fall into place. Everything would click and he wouldn't have any of these doubts and fears. But what did Violet know about all this?

'I'm not the guy for this,' he said quickly.

Rose seemed capable. From what Violet had told him Rose ran her life like clockwork. She never missed a deadline and made sure all those around her never missed one, too. He would only get in the way of someone like that.

Rose was standing in front of him. Her pale blue eyes fixed on his. 'Oh, yes, you are.' There was an edge to her voice. A determination he hadn't heard before.

But he recognised the trait. She was obviously her father's daughter.

'Oh, no, I'm not.'

Rose folded her arms across her chest. It was very unfortunate. All it did was emphasise her breasts in her pale yellow sundress. He could hardly tear his eyes away.

'Will Carter, you are not going to leave me in this mess.'

It felt as if the room were crowding around him. The walls, slowly but surely pushing forward. Sort of the way he normally felt when he knew he had to run from a wedding. None of this was his making. None of this was his responsibility.

'This isn't anything to do with me, Rose. It's bad enough that you cracked me over the head and scarred me for life with some vase. Now, you're trying to force me to help with your parents' wedding plans. This is nothing to do with me. Nothing at all. I'm far too busy for this. I've got a hundred other things to do to get publicity for my homeless charity. That's where I need to focus my efforts right now. Not on some celebrity wedding.' He flicked his hand, and she narrowed her gaze.

She was mad. And not just a little.

'Don't you give me any of your crap.' She poked her finger into his chest. 'You slunk your way into my bed uninvited. You've forced me to be around you for the next twenty-four hours when I should be working. I'm good at my job, Will. I manage my commitments. But this? On top of everything else I've got to do? I know nothing about weddings. Nothing. Ask me to design the jewellery—fine. Ask me to do anything else? I don't have a clue.' She poked his chest again. 'Which is where you come in.'

She lifted her chin and gave him a smug smile. 'You want publicity for your homeless charity? Oh, I can get you publicity. I can get you publicity in ways you might never even have imagined. But it comes at a price.'

Boy, she could look fierce when she wanted to. He wondered whatever happened to any guy that crossed her. He could barely begin to imagine.

'Weddings give me cold sweats,' he said quickly.

'Weddings have you running for the hills,' she countered.

There was no way she was going to back down. He was beginning to regret virtually blackmailing her into coming back to his house for twenty-four hours. Somehow him doing the blackmailing didn't seem quite so bad as her doing it back.

That would teach him.

But something happened. Rose seemed to change tack. A smile appeared on her face and she reached over and rubbed his arm. 'This one won't require you to break out in a cold sweat, Will. You're safe. This is someone else's wedding you're organising—not your own.' The smile stayed fixed on her face. He had a sneaking suspicion she was used to getting her own way.

But something was burning away underneath. It didn't matter that the face was identical to his best friend's. The personality and actions were totally different. She even smelled different. And her scent was currently winding its way around his senses. Something fruity. Something raspberry.

She flicked her blonde hair over her shoulder and he got another waft. Shampoo. It must be her shampoo. Rose Huntingdon-Cross was a knockout. And he was in danger of being bitten by her quirky charm. Her words had already captured his attention but the image in front of him and that enticing scent were in danger of doing much more.

He tried to focus. He needed PR for the homeless charity, he needed the rest of the world to understand why people ended up that way and help put in place things to prevent it.

'What exactly do you mean? Forget about the wedding stuff. Tell me about your PR ideas.'

She wagged her finger at him. 'Oh, no. Not

yet. You have to earn the privilege of my PR expertise. You help me, and I'll help you.'

What mattered more to him? Giving some crazy recommendations for caterers or wedding cars—or raising the profile of the charity he supported? There was no question. Of course he could do this. It couldn't possibly take that long. Rose looked like the kind of girl who could make a decision quickly. With wedding planning that was half the battle. Maybe this wouldn't be as bad as he thought?

She was biting her lip now, obviously worried he wouldn't agree. Biting a pink, perfectly formed lip. Perfectly formed for kissing. It was the thing that finally tipped him. Rose looked vulnerable. And he was a sucker for damsels in distress. It had got him into a whole lot of trouble in the past and probably would in the future.

His impulses got the better of him. He reached forward and grabbed her hand. 'Right, you've got a deal. Now, let's go before your parents appear again and give you something else to do.'

'You'll help me? Really?' He could almost hear her sigh of relief. 'Fabulous!' She was practically skipping alongside him as they crossed the room.

What on earth was he getting into?

Her brain was spinning. The guys from Will's place had packed up her gear in their van. She'd run after her parents and tried to get them to answer a few basic questions—like a date. But that had been fruitless. Apparently everything was up to her. They just wanted to decide on the guests.

The journey in the car to Will's place had been brief while she'd scribbled frantic notes in her handy black planner. She didn't go anywhere without that baby. He'd spent most of his time on the phone talking business. Then they'd turned down a country road that seemed to go on and on for ever.

Then, all of a sudden they were driving alongside a dark blue lake with an island in the middle, all sitting in front of a huge country house. The driver pulled up outside and she turned to him as he pushed his phone back into his pocket.

'You own a lake? And an island?' Her jaw was practically bouncing off her knees. Rose had been lucky. She'd had a privileged background. She was used to country mansions and houses costing millions. Seb's castle had just about topped everything. But this place?

Wow. The house might not be so big. But the amount of land was enormous. Will Carter was sitting on a gold mine.

'You like?' He was smiling at her amazed expression as she climbed out of the car.

The wind had picked up a little and was making her dress flap around her. She stepped around the car and walked towards the lake. There was a wooden jetty with two expensive boats sitting next to it.

She shook her head. 'Violet never mentioned a lake, or an island.' She thought she knew her sister well. This was definitely the kind of thing she would normally mention.

Will walked up behind her, blocking the wind. Her first thought was relief. Her next was how close he was standing. The soft cotton of his T-shirt was brushing against her shoulder blades.

In any other set of circumstances she would step away. But for the first time in a long time, she didn't feel like that. She was comfortable around Will. They might have got off to a bad start but there was something safe about him. It didn't help that the driver had just magically disappeared.

And it was easier to think safe than sexy. Because that was the other thought circulating around in her brain.

Will Carter was more than a little handsome. He was tongue-hanging-out, drip-your-food-down-your-dress handsome.

'Violet was never that interested in the lake or the island. She wouldn't even let me take her over in the boat.' His deep voice, right next to her ear, made her start.

'Oh, sorry. Did I give you a fright?' His arm slid naturally to her hip, to stop her from swaying. And she didn't mind it there. She naturally turned her head towards his and gave her full attention to the dark blue rim around his paler blue eyes. It was unusual. It was almost mesmerising.

'No,' she murmured, giving the slightest shake of her head.

This was freaking her out. She could feel her heart miss a few beats as she made the association. Last time she'd paid this much attention to a man had been over three years ago.

Three years ago and a party. A party where she'd left her friend to her own devices—because she'd been distracted by that man. Her friend had made some bad decisions that night and paid the ultimate price. And Rose had spent the last three years in New York to get away from the fallout.

She'd still spoken to her sisters every day and had been back in England every year for their father's annual rock concert, but she just hadn't stayed for long. It was easier to avoid the same circle of friends and their whispers if you weren't there to notice them.

But things were changing. It was looking as though a move back to England was on the cards. The European tour would need her close at hand. It would be just as easy to do the rest of her work here as in New York. The annual rock concert was due to take place soon and as long as she had equipment she could make her wedding jewellery anywhere.

'Rose?'

Will reached over and slid his hand in hers. 'Come on, I'll take you over to the island.'

He gave her hand a little tug. Oh, no. There was a warm feeling racing up her arm, making her heart rate do strange things. Pitter-pattering and electric shock kind of things.

She was trying to be cool. She was trying so hard to be cool. But his touch brought a natural smile to her face. She couldn't stop the little edges of her mouth turning upwards. 'Sure,' she said as he pulled her towards the boat.

It was one of two moored on a little wooden jetty and it certainly wasn't your old-fashioned rowing boat. It was white and sleek with a small compact engine on the back.

He jumped down and held out his hand towards her as the boat wobbled on the rippling surface of the water.

She leaned forward and hesitated a little. The step to the boat was a little broader than normal; chances were she would have to pull up her dress to make it across.

But it was almost as if Will read her mind. He reached forward with his long arms, circled her waist and lifted her across. He did it so quickly she didn't even have time to think. Her feet touched the base of the boat as the momentum made it sway a little more.

'Sorry.' He smiled. 'Forgot about your dress. Don't want to get a glimpse of anything I shouldn't.' He had that twinkle in his eye again—knowing full well he'd more or less glimpsed the full package this morning. *As had she.*

She sat down on one of the comfortable leather seats in the boat and shook her head. 'My grandmother would love you—but you're just full of it, aren't you? I often wondered if Mr Charming might be a journalist's daydream. I always wondered how you managed to stay on the good side of the media. But you're just every mother's dream, aren't you?'

He started the engine and laughed. 'I think I can name at least four mothers who don't like me that much at all.'

The boat moved easily across the peaceful lake. It really was perfect. A few swans were gathered at the other side and a few ducks squawked from the edges amongst the reeds.

Rose couldn't help but shake her head. 'I don't get it. I just don't. You must have known you didn't want to marry those girls. Why on earth would you leave it to the last minute? Who does that?'

He sat down next to her as he steered the boat. He wasn't as defensive as before. Maybe because they'd been around each other a bit longer. He'd seen the fix her parents had just left her with.

He sighed as the boat chugged across the water. 'I know. It's awful. And I don't mean to—I never do. And, to be fair, I've had bad press. I've only *actually* done it on the day once. It's just much more fun for the press to label me the Runaway Groom on every occasion. My problem is I always start to have doubts. Doubts that you can't say out loud without hurting the person you're with. The would-she-still-love-me-if-I'm-bankrupt? kind of doubts. Then, you start planning the wedding and the lovely woman you've fallen in love with is replaced by a raging, seething perfectionist.'

Rose laughed. 'What's wrong with that? Doesn't every bride want her day to be perfect? And don't most people have a few doubts in the lead-up to a wedding?'

But Will looked sad. 'But why does it all have to be about the details? Shouldn't it just be about two people in love getting married? Why does the wedding planning always turn into "this wedding has to be better than such and such's wedding"? I hate that.'

The words sent a little chill over her skin. He was right. More than he could ever know. She couldn't believe that the man the press called the Runaway Groom actually felt the same way she did.

'Why do you have doubts?' she asked quickly.

He paused and shrugged his shoulders. 'I'm not always sure. What I can tell you is that I don't regret calling off any of my weddings. I just regret the one time of being an actual runaway groom. At least two of my exes have since agreed that we should never have got married. They've met their perfect person and are happy now.'

Rose gave a sad kind of smile. 'Not every wedding is a disaster. Some couples are meant to be together. Daisy's wedding was fast, but she did plan everything she wanted. I might have been in New York but she emailed every day.' The island was getting closer, giving little hints of what lay beneath the copse of trees. She gave a little shudder. 'I'm not a fan of big weddings. I like small things. And I like the idea of two people, alone, agreeing to spend the rest of their lives together. Let's face it. That's what it's all about.' She smiled at Will. 'Just as well I'm not the bride. If it was a big, flamboyant wedding maybe I would steal your thunder and be the Runaway Bride?'

He leaned back a little in the boat as they neared the island's jetty. 'Really? A woman that wants a quiet wedding? Even after all the splendour of Daisy's?' He raised his eyebrows in disbelief. 'You don't want a little of that for yourself?'

'Absolutely not.' Her answer was definite.

He paused for a second. 'It really wasn't about the weddings. It was about the relationships. Once the initial happy buzz of being engaged vanished I started trying to picture myself growing old with that person. And no matter how hard I tried, I could never see it. I realised I didn't love them the way I should. The way a husband should love a wife—like your mum and dad.' He was gazing off onto the island and he suddenly realised what he'd said. Will Carter had probably revealed much more than he wanted to. He gave a little start and tried to change the subject quickly. 'Anyway, I don't believe you. I bet you want the big wedding just like every other girl.'

He stood up as the boat bumped the jetty and tied the mooring line securely. He jumped onto the wooden platform and she held out her hand to his. But Will seemed to think they'd set a precedent. He reached both arms down and caught her around the waist, lifting her up alongside him.

Her feet connected with the wooden structure but his hands didn't move from her waist. She was facing his chest, his head just above hers. Her hands lifted naturally to rest on his muscled biceps. The only noise was the quacking ducks and rippling water. She'd seen a little glimpse of the real Will Carter. Not the one in the media. Not Mr Charming. And she actually liked it. She would never admit it to anyone but he intrigued her. She smiled. 'No, I don't want any of that. What's more, I bet I could outrun you, Will Carter.' Her voice was quiet, almost a whisper. It was just the two of them. And their position was so close it seemed almost intimate. She could feel his fingers spread a little on her waist—as if he were expanding his grip to stop her getting away.

The perfect smile appeared, quickly followed by his dimple. It was all she could do not to reach out and touch it. 'The Runaway Bride and the Runaway Groom? We could be quite a pair.' He left his words hanging in the air. Leaving them both to contemplate them.

Her breath was caught in her throat. Never. She was too young. Too stupid. She had too many plans. There was no room for someone like Will Carter in her life right now. Especially when she found it so hard to trust her instincts. Her stomach flipped over. He was joking. They both were. But she couldn't help but feel a little surge of confidence that he'd even suggested it.

She stepped back, breathing deeply and breaking the intimate atmosphere between them. 'What's on this island anyway?'

Something flitted across his eyes. Disappointment? She felt a tiny surge of annoyance. She'd no intention of being his next passing fling. He'd already admitted he fell in love too easily. Rose didn't have that problem. She'd never fallen in love at all.

Ever the gentleman, he gestured with his hand to the path ahead leading through some trees. She walked ahead of him and looked around. The thick, dark trees were deceiving. They were hiding more than she could ever have imagined.

Her hand came up to her mouth as they stepped out from the path to a red-brick stone church with a huge stained-glass window.

'A hidden church? You have got to be joking.'

'No.' He walked over and swung open the thick wooden door, flicking a switch. The sun was shining down through the dark copse of trees. The church was tiny, the window almost taking up one whole wall. Only around twenty people could fit in here along the four benches on each side of the aisle.

The late afternoon sun was streaming through the window, sending a beautiful array of colours lighting up the white walls. There was a dark wooden altar table at the front. Nothing else.

'This place is amazing. You own a church?'

He nodded. 'There's an equally tiny cottage behind the church. Both were ruins when I bought the place. I had the church rebuilt and the stained-glass window put in. The cottage was just refurbished.'

She spun around in the rainbow of lights. 'I love this place. What was it originally?'

'No one really knows for sure. I think it was some kind of retreat. There used to be a monastery on these grounds right up until the dissolution of the monasteries in the fifteen-hundreds. This is the only thing that was left.'

Rose took a deep breath and walked over and touched the white wall. 'Think of all the history here. Think of all the things that could have happened between these four walls over the centuries.' She walked over and gently touched one of the pieces of stained red glass as she swept her eyes over the scene in the window. 'What is this? Was there something like this already here?'

'It's inspired by Troyes Cathedral in France. They have some of the oldest medieval stained-glass windows. This is two of the prophets, Moses and David.' He seemed genuinely interested in what he was telling her. It was obvious a lot of thought—and a lot of expense—had gone into the restoration work.

'You should get a grant of approval to do wedding ceremonies here.'

He shook his head. 'What? And have the bride fall out of the boat on the way over? This lake might look pretty but, I can assure you, it's dark and murky at the bottom.'

She laughed and stepped closer. 'Words from a man that sounds like he fell in.'

'I did. I came out like a creature from the black lagoon.'

She held out her hands. 'So what do you use this place for?' She finally felt as if she was getting to know Will a little better. He might be Mr Charming for the press but he was also a nice guy. He was easier to be around than she'd first experienced. Violet wasn't known for her poor judgement. She should have trusted her sister.

He waved her forward. 'Come and I'll show you.'

They walked outside and behind the church to a whitewashed cottage with black paint around the windows and a black door. He pushed it open and showed her inside.

It was tiny, but spectacular. Almost every part was in view. An open modern kitchen at one end, a sitting area in the middle and a platform with a king-sized bed. There was even a smoky glass bricked wall, which hid the wash-hand basin and toilet, but the roll-top bath was placed in front of one of the two windows.

'You bathe at the window!' Rose's mouth dropped open.

Will grinned. 'It's all private. If someone is staying here, the island is all theirs. No one else can set foot on the place. Total privacy. People like that.'

It was just the way he said the words. They were happy, nonchalant. But as they left his mouth she tried to picture who would want to get away from everything. There was no obvious TV, no phone and she doubted there would be an Internet signal.

'Who comes here, Will? Do you hire it out?'

He shook his head. 'Never. This place is for friends. For people who need a little time, a little space.'

She tilted her head to the side. She'd heard of places like this. One of the members of her dad's band had taken himself off to a mountain retreat a few years ago after numerous visits to rehab clinics. She sucked in a breath. Was this the kind of place she should have gone three years ago after her friend had died from the drug overdose?

This place was a sanctuary. A private hideaway from the world outside. It was perfect.

'Like your friend who was homeless?'

He was fighting an internal battle that played out on his tightly composed features. He gave a brief nod.

'I love it,' she whispered. 'I hope the people that come here find what they need.'

Will's hands appeared at her waist. She hadn't even realised he'd moved close to her. He exhaled sharply and she could feel his muscles relax behind her. 'That's so nice to hear you say. And it's why I don't bring people here—don't advertise the fact there's anything on this island.'

He was trusting her. He was trusting her not to say anything to the world outside. Something inside her chest fluttered.

All of a sudden she had a real awareness of the big bed on the platform behind her. It looked sumptuous. It looked inviting. They were here alone, on an island that no one else could reach. They wouldn't be disturbed.

'You don't bring people here?'

He shook his head. 'Never.' His voice was low, husky. It was sending blood racing through her veins.

Her head was swimming. She was crazy. She'd just met this guy. He might be her sister's best friend but she hardly knew him at all. Trouble was, everything she did know she liked.

Her hands rested on the warm skin of his muscled arms again, feeling the tickle of tiny hairs under the palms of her hands.

'Then why me?' Her throat felt scratchy. She was almost afraid to breathe.

Before she knew what she was doing she lifted one hand and touched his rumpled, slightly too long hair. With his dimple and killer blue eyes all he needed was a white coat and he could easily replace that actor from the lastest TV hospital show.

His head tilted slightly towards her hand as she ran her fingers through his hair, holding her breath. What on earth was she doing?

Her mouth was dry and she had a strong urge for some of the leftover wine from her sister's wedding. Last night she'd just been too exhausted to have even more than two glasses.

Will didn't seem to object to her touch. He responded instantly, stepping forward and firming his gentle grip on her waist. His face was only inches from hers. She could feel his breath on her cheek. She could see the tiny, almost invisible freckles on the bridge of his nose, the tiny lines around his eyes. Her mouth was wet and she ran her tongue across her lips. They tingled. All the pores of her skin lifted up in a soft carpet of goosebumps, each hair on her body standing up and tingling at the roots. She'd never experienced anything like this before.

He didn't bring people here—but he'd brought her. What did that mean? She had absolutely no idea.

'I thought you might like it. Might appreciate it the way others wouldn't. I was right.'

Her head was telling her to back away, to break their gaze and step out of his hold. Her brain was befuddled. She'd learned not to trust her instincts. She'd learned to question everything. But Will moved forward, the hard planes of his chest and abdomen pressing against her breasts, his hands sliding downward and tilting her pelvis towards his.

His words were like a drug. As an independent woman Rose had never craved a man's approval before. But suddenly Will Carter liking her, respecting her, seemed like the most important thing on earth.

This was it. Enough. It was time to step away. This man had led enough women on a merry dance. She wasn't about to be the next.

But her body wasn't listening to her brain.

Neither of them had spoken for the last few seconds. Any minute now he'd step away and she'd feel like a fool. She was sleep deprived—that was what was wrong.

Even though she'd gone to bed at midnight and slept soundly until this morning she was still on New York time. It was making her do strange things. It was making her act in ways that she wouldn't normally.

Will blinked. His gaze was hypnotic. She couldn't pull herself away. She didn't want to—no matter what her brain said.

'I don't just like it,' she whispered. 'I love it.' It was true. This place felt safe. Felt private. Like a complete and utter haven where two people could suspend disbelief and do anything they wanted.

She moistened her lips as his gaze lowered to her mouth.

He reached up a finger and brushed a strand of hair away from her face. His touch like butterfly wings on her skin. She bit her swollen lips. As he moved forward his scent enveloped her. Pure and utter pheromones. She couldn't get enough of them.

It was her last thought as Will Carter's lips came into contact with hers.

CHAPTER FOUR

FOR A FEW seconds he was lost. Lost in the smell of her. Lost in the taste of her. And lost in the surge of hormones that were rushing around his body.

He was engulfed in the wave of restless energy floating through the air between them, colliding like seismic waves. Someplace, somewhere the Richter scale was measuring the magnitude between them.

It was great. *She* was great. His hands skirted over her curves, his fingers brushing against her silky skin. A groan escaped from the back of his throat as every body part acted accordingly.

Then, from out of nowhere, a voice echoed in his head. *Runaway groom my sister and I'll kill you.*

It brought him back to his senses, back to reality. Violet would kill him. There was no doubt.

He stepped back, leaving Rose's lips mid-kiss and her eyes still shut. She was frozen for the tiniest of seconds in that position before her startled eyes opened.

He was trying to catch his ragged breath. Trying not to still taste her on his lips.

Their gazes collided and he saw a million things flash through her eyes. Confusion. Embarrassment. Lust.

He lifted his hands and shook his head. 'Rose, I'm so sorry. I should never have done that. I just… I just…' He couldn't find the words—probably because his brain was completely scrambled. He walked over to the edge of the bed and sat down, running his fingers through his hair. The same motion that she'd been doing only seconds earlier.

Bad idea. Very bad idea. She looked even more confused now. He threw up his hands. 'It's this place. Here, and the church.' She still hadn't said a word. But the expression on her face was killing him. Violet really would kill him if her sister told her about this.

'I never meant for this to happen. I didn't plan it.'

'Obviously.' It was her first word and it was as cold as ice. The beautiful ambient temperature had just dropped by about twenty degrees.

'No. That's not what I mean. You're beautiful. You're more than beautiful. And your smell. And your curves. I just…'

The initial glare disappeared and the corners of her mouth started to turn upwards. His babbling must be amusing her. But he couldn't help it. He always got like this when he'd blundered. Why say three words when you could say twenty?

She stepped forward so that the fabric of her dress was almost touching his nose. It was swaying gently. He was trying not to think what was underneath. Or about the feel of her skin.

She sighed. 'Will, do I make you nervous?' He couldn't miss the hint of amusement in her voice.

He looked up. She was close, oh, so close. Her scent was there again.

'Yes…I mean no. Well, maybe.'

She folded her arms across her chest. 'How about we just file this away somewhere? You're Violet's best friend and…' she raised her eyebrows '…you have just about the worst reputation on the planet. I'm never going to get involved with a guy like you.'

'You're not?' He couldn't help it. Defence was the instant reaction to her words. What was so wrong with him anyway? Okay, he might have been engaged a few times but he was a good guy. Really, he was.

She was definitely smiling now. He should be relieved. He should be thankful. So why was he feeling a little insulted?

'No. I'm definitely not.' She turned and walked

over to the window. 'Why don't we just chalk this up to a moment of madness? I need you to help me with the wedding stuff. You need me to help with your publicity. We can do this, can't we? We can spend the next few weeks around each other and forget that this ever happened.'

It wasn't a question. It was a statement of fact. She was right. He knew she was right. But Will had never had problems getting a woman before. Rose telling him outright *no* was a bit of a revelation for him.

He stood up and touched his head. She was trying to brush this off. The easiest thing in the world to do was let her. 'Why don't we just pin it down to my head injury?' He was teasing her. Hinting that she'd caused the whole thing.

But Rose was far too quick for him. She laughed. 'Are you trying to make out I've taken advantage of the person I'm supposed to be looking after? What does that make me?'

'A ruthless businesswoman.'

She smiled. She seemed to like that, then something flitted across her eyes and she glanced at her watch. 'Will? Weren't you supposed to have a business meeting this afternoon?'

Recognition flooded through him. 'Oh, no. What time is it? Darn it.'

She shook her head and opened the door.

'We've got five minutes. We can make it in that time, can't we?'

'Let's run.' He grabbed her hand as he jogged past and pulled the door closed behind them. It only took a minute to run along the path to the boat and he started the engine quickly. Rose didn't wait to be helped into the boat. She lifted her skirt up, giving him a complete flash of her bronzed legs as she jumped over the gap between the jetty and the boat. The boat rocked furiously as she landed and he grabbed her around the waist and pushed her into one of the seats.

The boat crossed the water in a few minutes. This meeting was important. He had to make it on time. But his eyes kept skimming across to Rose. Her blonde hair was streaking behind her in the wind and her yellow dress outlined her curves again.

He groaned. How on earth was he going to manage the next few weeks?

The football player was every bit as sleazy as she remembered. He'd practically sneered once Will had introduced her and he'd clicked about who her father was. But Rose couldn't have cared less. She'd work to do.

Her jewellery equipment had arrived and with the help of two of Will's staff she'd set it up quickly and spent a few hours putting the finishing touches to the two wedding rings.

'Rose, are you in here?'

She looked up from giving the rings a final polish. Will crossed the room in a few steps, smiling as usual. 'I see you managed to get things set up. How's it going?'

She held up the rings encased in their black velvet boxes. 'I've just finished. The courier will be here to pick them up in the next hour. What do you think?'

He bent forward and moved her Anglepoise light to get a better look at the intricate mix of rose and yellow gold for the bride's ring, and solid white gold for the groom's. She could see the flicker of surprise on his face.

'Rose, these are beautiful. You made these from scratch? Yourself? How on earth did you know where to start?'

She sighed and leaned back. 'Did you think I was pretending to make jewellery?'

He shook his head, obviously realising his mistake. 'No, I didn't mean it like that, it's just...' Then he stopped. And smiled. And sat down next to her.

'How do you do that to me?'

She couldn't help but grin. She knew exactly what was coming but she put on her most innocent expression. 'Do what, exactly?'

He shrugged his shoulders. 'Make me start babbling like some teenage boy. I always seem to say the wrong thing around you, then can't find the words to straighten things out.'

She raised her eyebrows. 'I thought you said I didn't make you nervous.'

He frowned. 'Well, you don't. But then—you do.' He flung up his hands. 'See, I don't know.'

She laughed. 'How did your business meeting go with El Creepo?'

His mouth fell open and his shoulders started shaking. 'El Creepo? That's what you're calling him?'

She nodded sombrely and folded her arms. 'I think it suits him.'

'I think you might be right.' He ran his fingers through his hair, carefully avoiding his stitched forehead. Guilt surged through her again. It had to be sore, but he hadn't complained at all. 'But at the moment he's the best bet I've got. You're right. There's just something about him I can't put my finger on. But if it's the only way to raise publicity then what choice do I have?'

Sitting in such close proximity to Will, she could see the tiny lines around his eyes and on his forehead. He was genuinely worried about this. He was genuinely trying to do some good. How far would he go?

She bit her lip. 'I might have some alternative ideas about that.'

'For the publicity?'

'Yes.' She rubbed her hands on her dress. It was warm in this room. Her soldering equipment gave out a lot of heat, which only made it worse. And she couldn't wait to actually hit the shower and change her clothes.

'Tell me more.'

She shook her head. 'Not yet, and you still have to hold your side of the bargain.' She stood up. 'I want to get changed and have a shower but I don't have any of my things.'

He looked a little sheepish. 'Actually you do. Violet sent your bright blue case over. I take it you'll have everything you need in there? Why don't you freshen up and we can have some dinner?'

Violet had sent her case over? Just like that? Just wait until she spoke to her sister. She'd better not be trying to matchmake.

She gave a little nod of her head just as Will's eyes twinkled and his smile broadened to reveal his dimples. Darn it. Those were the last things she needed to see right now.

'Now, I'm only showing you to a room in my house if you promise not to cause any damage.'

He was waiting for her at the door. 'Do you

keep any ancient vases in your rooms?' she quipped.

'Not in yours,' he countered.

'Any unidentified men crawling into bed with perfect strangers?'

His gaze met hers. 'Only if requested.'

Her breath caught in her throat as her skin prickled involuntarily. Oh, boy, he was good. She had to keep remembering just how many times this guy had been attached. Still, dinner at Gideon Hall might actually be quite nice. Rose was as nosey as the next person and always liked to see around beautiful homes.

Will led her up the large curved staircase and along a corridor. Everything was sparkling. Everything was clean. Everything was cream.

He swung open the door of one room and she stepped inside. Finally, a tiny bit of colour. Pale yellow to complement the cream. It was gorgeous. She couldn't help but walk straight across to touch the ornate curtains. Curtains and soft furnishings had always been her weakness. It was like something from one of those classy house magazines. An enormous bed with soft bedding and cushions that just invited you to dive in, pale yellow wallpaper with tiny flowers, a pale yellow carpet and light-coloured furniture all leading to large windows looking over the gardens.

'These are beautiful. The whole place is beautiful.' She smiled wickedly. 'Which one of your brides-to-be helped you decorate?'

'Actually, some of it I chose myself. Others, I had some help from professionals.' He straightened a little more and his chest puffed out. He was obviously pleased with the backhanded compliment.

'Really?' She was surprised. She'd just imagined that he'd waved his hand and asked someone else to sort all this out for him.

'Yes, really. Why does that seem strange?'

'It just does, that's all.'

'It's strange that a guy is interested in how his home looks?'

She paused. When he said it out loud it didn't seem so strange. She just couldn't imagine Will Carter sitting with a dozen sample books and picking wallpaper and soft furnishings.

She walked over and stuck her head into the white bathroom with pale yellow towels. Everything matching perfectly. 'Okay, maybe not.'

He gave a little nod. As if he was pleased he'd won the argument. 'How about I leave you to freshen up and we meet downstairs later for dinner?' He hesitated. 'Is there anything you don't like? Any allergies?'

She shook her head. 'I'll let you into a secret. I'm a simple girl. Chicken is my favourite no matter what you do to it.'

He looked relieved. 'I can definitely do chicken.' He glanced towards the window again. 'How do you feel about sitting outside? We could have dinner on the patio overlooking the gardens and the lake.'

Her insides gave a little flutter. This was starting to sound a lot more like a date than a business meeting. And even though it was wrong—even though she'd already told Will he would never be for her—it was still flattering.

The last few years had been hard. She wasn't the party girl she'd been before. She'd been used to flirting and high-speed dating. As soon as she'd bored of one guy, she'd moved on to the next—none of them serious.

But everything had changed after Autumn's death. They'd been friends for a few years and had liked socialising together. When Rose had left the party with the man of the moment she'd assumed Autumn was fine, too. An assumption that was completely wrong. She'd been foolish. And partly to blame. Even though Rose had never dabbled with drugs herself she'd known that Autumn did so on occasion. But Autumn was independent and strong-willed. Telling her not to do something was practically impossible. But the guilt Rose felt was still overwhelming. If she'd been there, she would have noticed Autumn was unwell. Her friend wouldn't have been found slumped in a corner and not breathing. She could have called an ambulance and intervened.

Instead a few hours later she'd heard her dad's scratchy voice on the phone demanding to know where she was and if she was okay. Rose had known straight away something was wrong. Her parents were very liberal and once the girls had reached the age of twenty-one they could pretty much do what they wanted. By the grand old age of twenty-four she should have known so much better. She'd never forgotten the look on his face as she'd pulled up in a taxi outside Huntingdon Hall. He'd been standing in the doorway watching for her while her mother was sitting inside waiting to tell her the news.

Drug deaths were always good media fodder. And Rose had found herself the unwitting angle for every story.

Pop star's daughter at drug party.

Wild child Rose Huntingdon-Cross's friend dies of drug overdose.

After the funeral she hadn't been able to get out of the country quick enough. Dealing with PR was the last thing she'd wanted to do. But it went hand in hand with the job for her dad's band. She'd learned who to talk to, who to ignore and who to threaten to sue. All valuable skills in this life.

Skills she was going to exploit to help Will

Carter get what he wanted. She only hoped he'd listen to reason when she explained what she wanted to do. She smiled at him. 'Dinner outside would be lovely. Thanks. Give me an hour to get changed.'

He gave a little nod of his head and walked out, closing the door behind him. Leaving Rose staring out over the lake towards the island. She ran her hands up and down her arms. There was something about that place. Something magical. Something mystical. And there was no way she was ever setting foot there again with Will Carter.

Violet's sister. Violet's sister. He muttered the words under his breath all along the length of the corridor. If he kept reminding himself that he'd put the relationship with his best friend at risk if he ventured too near, he might actually convince himself.

He had to do something, because right now his head was full of *that kiss*.

The softness of her hair, the silkiness of her skin, the taste of her lips. Enough.

He had to stop this. Violet had warned him, and she almost knew him better than he knew himself. She knew he fell head over heels with the next beautiful woman to come along—suitable or not. And Rose was definitely *not* suitable.

But Rose wasn't like any of the others. He'd never felt compelled to take any of his fiancées to the island—none of them had ever shown much interest.

And none of them had ever had the same expression in their eyes that Rose had when he'd shown her into her room. It wasn't anything to do with wealth or prosperity; it was to do with making a house a home. Rose appreciated that. And he appreciated her because of it.

He walked down the wide staircase and into the kitchen where Judy, his housekeeper and chef all rolled into one, was waiting. 'What'll it be?' She smiled.

'Chicken. Do whatever you like with it, as long as it's chicken.'

She nodded. 'Well, that's easy. Do you want some dessert, too?'

Darn it. He hadn't even thought to ask. But Judy was used to him.

'How about some fresh fruit pavlova? I made some earlier for that grump of a football player but he didn't want any.'

Will gave a sigh of relief. 'Perfect.' He took a quick look around the kitchen. As usual everything was gleaming. The staff who worked here really took their jobs seriously. He was lucky to have them.

Judy started pulling ingredients from the huge

fridge. 'So, who is our guest, then? Anybody I should know?'

He shook his head quickly. 'It's nobody. It's just Violet's sister.'

Judy looked interested. 'Rose? I've heard Violet talk about her a lot but I've never met her before. Are they alike?'

He paused, not quite sure how to answer. Violet had never made the blood race back through his veins as Rose had. 'They look alike, but they're totally different people,' he said quickly. It seemed the simplest enough answer.

Judy gave a little nod of her head as she started slicing vegetables on a wooden board. 'I'll look forward to meeting her, then. Dinner will be ready in about forty minutes. Just give me a shout when you're ready.' She gave Will a little wink and he cringed. She always did that.

It was almost as if she could read his mind and see what he was really thinking.

Business. That was what this was. And if he kept that in his head he'd do fine. Weddings. He tried to stop the shiver going down his spine at the mere thought of it. He could write a list. That was what he'd do. He'd change his shirt, then write a list for Rose of the things she'd need to plan.

Anything to keep him on track.

* * *

Rose was used to luxury. Their family home certainly didn't scrimp on anything. Hawksley Castle had been something else entirely. But this place—Gideon Hall—added a whole new dimension.

It wasn't quite as big as Huntingdon Hall but it had more land—more space. And Will's taste was surprisingly good. The furnishings were comfortable but stylish. It had a show-home look about it, while still giving that you-could-actually-live-here feel.

She finished drying her hair and opened her suitcase to find some more clothes. It didn't take long. Clean underwear and a bright blue knee-length jersey dress. Even though the sun wasn't quite so high in the sky it was still hot outside and the last thing she wanted to do round about Will Carter was feel hot and bothered.

She gave a quick squirt of perfume, spent two minutes putting on some make-up and stuck on some flat, comfortable gold sandals. Done.

By the time she walked down the main staircase at Gideon Hall she was feeling like a new woman. It was amazing what a shower and change of clothes could do for a girl. Will was standing at the door to the huge kitchen. 'Rose, come and meet Judy. She's made dinner for us.'

Rose came into the kitchen and held her hand

out towards Judy. 'It's a pleasure to meet you. I hope you haven't gone to too much trouble for us.'

Judy beamed and shook her hand swiftly. 'You're so much like your sister. It's amazing. Do you ever get mistaken for each other?'

Will could see the tiniest flicker of something in Rose's face. She'd probably heard this for the best part of her twenty-seven years. And from most of the pictures he'd seen of Violet and Rose they normally tried to look a bit different—a bit more individual.

Rose touched her long, straight hair. 'We look alike more by default than anything deliberate. I've been in the States for the last few years. Violet and I always tried something different. I would be shorter, she would be longer. I would go lighter, she'd go darker. I'd be curls, she'd be straight. You get the picture.' She shrugged her shoulders. She fingered a lock of her blonde hair. 'I'll really need to do something with this.'

'Don't you dare.' The words were out before he knew it and both heads turned towards him with startled expressions on their faces. He gulped and let out his best attempt at a laugh. 'Oh, I was just joking. Will we have some wine? What would you prefer—white or red?'

'White, sparkling if you have any.' Both women exchanged an amused glance as Will felt himself bluster around the kitchen. Where was the darn sparkling wine when he needed it?

Judy pulled the chicken from the oven and the smell of bubbling chicken stock, tomatoes and spicy peppers swamped the kitchen. 'That smells great,' said Rose. 'Is there anything I can do to help?'

Judy waved her hand. 'Not at all. Give me two minutes and I'll plate up for you, then you can take it outside. The cutlery and napkins are already there.'

He finally managed to find a chilled bottle of wine and popped the cork before grabbing a couple of glasses. Rose stood waiting with two plates of piping hot food in her hands. 'Lead the way, Mr Carter, and I hope you're prepared for this business meeting we're about to have.'

He couldn't help but smile as he led her through the house and out through the wide open doors at the dining room. The table was positioned on the patio overlooking the gardens and lake. It only took a few moments to pour the wine and he sat across from her and raised his glass.

'To interesting bed companions.'

She grinned and clinked his glass. 'To things that go bump in the morning.'

This was such a bad idea. She knew it from the second they clinked glasses and she let the cold sparkling wine slide down her throat. How many times had he done this before? Had a woman sit with him overlooking the gardens for dinner? The house was spectacular. Judy's cooking was brilliant. And Will was looking at her with that twinkle in his eyes...

He pulled out a piece of paper from his back pocket. 'Here. I've made you a list.'

'A list of what?' She spun the paper around and looked at the printed list with the bold heading of Wedding Arrangements. She bit the inside of her cheek to stop herself from laughing. 'What? You have a ready-made template just sitting, waiting for use?'

His brow wrinkled and he waved his fork at her. 'Enough. If you want my help, you're going to have to stop with all the wedding jokes. I thought you might want it for that black planner of yours.'

She tilted her head to one side as she lifted her glass towards him. 'You're such a spoilsport.'

He lifted his hand to his head and feigned a flinch. 'I think I've already suffered quite enough at your hands.'

'How long are you going to keep this up?'

He couldn't hide his smirk. 'Let's see. Stitches come out in seven days—at least that long.'

'If I find another vase, I'm hitting you again.'

He leaned across the table towards her and hit

her with his million-watt grin. 'Oh, go on, Rose, play fair.'

She couldn't help but laugh. Even when he was annoying, Will Carter was still alarmingly cute. And handsome. And sexy.

She took a final bite of the chicken and glanced down at the list. 'Why do some of these have ticks?'

Will leaned back in his chair and started counting off on his fingers. 'Rose, you've no idea how easy you've got it. The biggest thing—the venue. Your parents have already said they want to do it at Huntingdon Hall. Easy.' He gave a little shrug. 'You really need to check numbers though. You'll need to ensure you get a big enough marquee for the grounds.'

She gulped. A marquee. Where on earth was she going to find one of those, big enough to accommodate wedding guests and available in less than four weeks just as they were coming into summer? She lifted her glass. 'I think I'm going to need some more wine. What else?'

He kept counting on his fingers. 'Wedding photographer you've got. Why would you use anyone but Daisy?'

She nodded. 'But what about the pics we want Daisy to be in?'

'Doesn't she have an assistant?'

Rose racked her brain. 'I'm not sure. I'll need to ask.'

Will continued. 'As for the flowers, it goes without saying that Violet will do them. Even if it does mean getting up to go to some flower market at three a.m.'

Rose nodded. Violet would be able to conjure up whatever concoction her mother wanted for the day. Sherry had a tendency to like beautiful, bright and exotic flowers rather than the quiet-style flowers she'd named her daughters after.

'So what does that leave?'

Will took a sip of wine. 'Band, celebrant—or whoever they want to say their vows to—caterers, décor, wedding favours, drinks and bar.' He wrinkled his nose. 'Will you need a children's entertainer? Or a nanny for the guests' kids? Cars?' He waved his hand. 'No, they're getting married at home.'

Rose felt her stomach start to lurch. He was saying this was easy, but it sounded anything but. 'I have a horrible feeling that both Mum and Dad will want to make an entrance. They'll probably leave by the back door and come back up the drive for the wedding in front of the guests.'

'So you will need cars?'

She picked up the pen sitting on the table and drew a thick black line through the word *Cars*. 'Absolutely not. With what I know is sitting in

Dad's garages? Between what Mum knows about, and what she doesn't, there will definitely be enough for her to pick something she likes to come up the driveway in. Surely it's not that big a deal?'

Will let out a laugh. 'Oh, you've got so much to learn in so little time.' His hand came casually across the table and touched hers. 'Are you really ready for this?'

In an instant her tongue was sticking to the roof of her mouth, the inside so dry a camel could be marching through it. A dozen little centipedes had just invaded her body and were racing their way up the inside of her arm and directly to her fluttering heart. It was a warm evening. She wasn't the least bit cold. But the heat currently shooting up her arm could light up this whole mansion house.

What on earth was wrong with her? She'd been on lots of dates. She'd had a few relationships. But she'd never felt any of the old thunderbolts and lightning. She'd always thought that was nonsense.

But it seemed as if her body was trying to tell her something else entirely.

When she'd got ready earlier she hadn't really been that concerned about what she was wearing or how she looked. But all of a sudden it felt as if her dress might be a little too clingy, a little too revealing. She could sense his eyes on her curves, following the slope of her hips and swell of her breasts. She sat up a little straighter.

Her brain kept trying to temper her body's responses. *Runaway Groom. He's the Runaway Groom. He's absolutely, definitely* not *for you.*

Was she ready for all this? Not a chance.

Will wasn't quite sure what was happening. He'd virtually face-planted himself into his last four relationships and engagements. He'd been swept along with the early joy and the passion.

But this was something else entirely.

All he wanted to do was reach across the table and grab her and kiss her. It didn't help that the world was plotting against him and the sun had started to dip slightly in the sky, silhouetting her figure and perfect blonde hair on her shoulders. Or, more importantly, highlighting her silky skin and waiting-to-be-kissed lips.

It was automatic. The thought made him lick his lips and he could swear he could still taste her from earlier. He pulled his hands back from hers and lifted the wine glass to his lips. Empty. Darn it. It seemed as if both of them had inexplicably dry mouths.

He made an attempt to focus on the list. *Out of bounds.* He had to keep saying it over and over in his head.

His eyes scanned down the list of wedding items. There. That would stop him. Nothing like a list of wedding to-dos to temper his libido.

'What about catering? Do you have anyone in mind?'

Rose visibly jerked in her chair. It was as if her brain had been circling in the same clouds as his. At least that was what he was hoping.

She groaned. 'Oh, no. That will be a nightmare. Mum and Dad are so fussy about food.'

'You can't pull any special favours?'

She shook her head. 'I've already pulled special favours for the tour. And that was only to cater for five members of the band. We don't even know how many people they're inviting yet but I can guarantee you—it won't be five.'

Will frowned. 'It's such short notice. I hate to say it but you might need to take what you can get.'

'Oh, don't say that.' Rose put her head on the table, her blonde hair flicking up dramatically behind her. He smiled. She might appear calm on the surface but when the moment occurred it appeared that Rose could do drama.

He frowned. 'There's a conference on Monday at the Newbridge Auditorium. It's for businesses but there are always lots of caterers in attendance, trying to tout for business at events.'

She lifted her head just a little from the table.

He could only see one eye beneath the long locks. 'Catering for a business event isn't even in the same league as catering for a wedding.'

He arched his eyebrow at her. 'You'd be surprised. Some of these events have cordon bleu chefs. Again—numbers might be an issue. And you'll need to have some idea of a menu. Do you know what they like?'

'That's easy. Mum likes chicken and Dad will want steak with all the trimmings. But it has to taste just right.'

'Like mother, like daughter?'

She straightened in her chair. 'Yeah, I guess so. Though in most things I'm most like my dad.' She picked up a pencil. 'Dessert will need to be something chocolate for Mum—usually with orange—and anything with strawberries or raspberries for Dad.'

She screwed up her nose as she studied the list. 'Balloons, seat covers, wedding gifts, evening favours, wedding cake, hors d'oeuvres, and a bar.' Her head thumped back on the table. 'I can't do all this!'

Will reached over and grabbed her hand, this time propelling her from her chair and pulling her towards him. She barely had time to think about it before he plunked her down on his knee and wrapped his arm around her waist. 'I'm helping you. That's what the deal is. By Monday night we will have a caterer. By Tuesday we'll have sorted the chair covers, balloons and favours. If you pay enough you can pretty much get what you want.'

He stood up and turned her around in his arms, reaching up to touch her cheek, trying not to drink in the feel of her. 'Rose, stop worrying. I've already told you—the biggest things are sorted.' Her hands had moved automatically to his waist, her fingers gently pressing through his shirt. He wanted them to move. He wanted to feel them stroke across the expanse of his back and shoulders. He wanted to feel them running up the planes of his chest and wrap around his neck. If they could just move a little closer…

She was staring up at him with those big blue eyes. It made his breath catch in his throat. She'd never looked so beautiful. And for a second he was sure she was looking at him exactly the way that he was looking at her.

But then she blinked. And it was as if something had just flicked on in her brain. 'Yes, because you know all about this stuff, don't you?' Her hands fell from his sides and she took a step back.

What had just happened?

He gave himself an internal shake. 'Okay. Sit down. I'll go and get some of Judy's pavlova for us and some coffee. Then you can tell me all about your PR ideas for my homeless charity. Fair's fair.'

He picked up the plates and gave her a smile as he headed back inside. It only took a few minutes to be out of her sight and he stopped and pressed his head against the cool corridor wall. What was he thinking?

He was going to have to put a No Touching sign on her head.

Because if he didn't—he'd get himself into a whole load of trouble.

The pavlova looked magnificent, with lots of layers of gooey meringue, lashings of fresh cream and oodles of strawberries, raspberries and kiwi fruit. A girl might think she was in heaven. That, followed by the smell of rich coffee, was making her already full stomach think it might have to squeeze a little more inside.

She was ready. She was prepared. She'd taken the few moments of Will's absence to gather herself. A quick dash to the bathroom and a splash of water on her face and wrists had cooled her down. Technically speaking. It hadn't stopped that crazy irregular pattern inside her chest that she was trying to ignore.

Now, she was in control. And Will was back to his amiable, joking self. No more hot looks of what might be. No lingering glances or widening pupils.

'So what's the plan for PR?'

His voice sounded so calm, so laid-back. Now was the time to find out if he really was.

She savoured the last mouthful of pavlova and set down her fork. Her words were simple and she said them as if they were the most obvious thing in the world. 'The plan, Will—is you.'

He wrinkled his nose. 'What?'

She waved her hand. 'I didn't know you were associated with that homeless charity until you told me. And then I asked myself why. Because you've had more than enough media coverage in your time.'

He gave a shake of his head. 'But that was all the wedding stuff. It was all personal. It doesn't really count.'

She shook her head and leaned towards him. He really didn't get it. 'But that's just it, Will. *You're* the story. *You're* the person people want to read about. People love you. Your reputation as the Runaway Groom precedes you and it's time to use it to your advantage.'

The frown seemed to be spreading across his face. 'No. I don't agree. I hate all that stuff. How on earth can being known as the Runaway Groom help a homeless charity?'

She took a deep breath. It was obvious he was

going to take some persuading. 'You've seen all the TV shows with phone-in voting?'

He nodded warily. 'Yes, all the wannabe pop-star stuff?'

'Exactly. They often have the same things in newspapers. Vote for your favourite TV soap star. Vote for your favourite model.'

He was nodding slowly. 'I still don't get it. What does that have to do with me?'

She gave him her best PR smile. 'We're going to do something similar with you.'

He was shaking his head again. 'Why on earth would anyone vote for me?'

Rose sucked in a deep breath and talked quickly. 'People love the fact you were the Run-away Groom. Imagine we had a number of trials or dares for you to do. All hideous. All things that people would cringe at. We can ask the public to vote on which of them you should do for the homeless charity—earning money and raising awareness along the way.'

'But why on earth would people be interested in that?'

This was it. This was when she finally revealed her master stroke.

'Because there'll be four separate possibilities. All set by each of your jilted brides.'

'What?'

Rose jumped in quickly before he had too

much time to think about it. 'Just think about it. I bet some of them still want revenge on you. They'll probably take great pleasure in making a hideous suggestion for a dare. And I can spin it. From what you've told me, each one of your brides-to-be were interested in being in the media. If I pitch it to them as an opportunity to take a bit of revenge on you—plus the fact the money will be going to charity *and* you'll have to do whatever the winning dare is—I'm sure they'll take part. What's more the press will eat it up.'

Will's head had been shaking from the second she started speaking. His face wasn't pale as if he were shocked—it was starting to go red as if she'd made him angry. 'You have got to be joking. *This? This* is your plan?'

She shifted in her chair. 'If you'll just take a minute to consider it…'

He stood up sharply and his chair flew backwards. 'Take a minute? Take a minute to consider humiliating myself in front of millions? Have people talk about me instead of the charity? I'd be a laughing stock.'

Rose stayed as cool as she could. She lifted her coffee cup and took a sip as if guys shouting at her happened every day. In New York it wasn't that unusual and she was made of sterner stuff.

'Yes, you would,' she said simply. 'But people

would be interested to know why you were doing it. Why the world's most eligible bachelor would put himself through it. That would lead them to the homeless charity.'

His fists were clenched and pressing down on the table. She could see the flicker of an angry tic in his jaw. But after a few moments his breathing seemed to ease and the flush in his face died down. Rose sat quietly, sipping her coffee and looking out over the view.

This was the perfect solution to his PR problems. It had come to her earlier on and she'd known he wouldn't like it. But if he was as committed to the charity as he claimed to be, he'd realise just how much this could work.

He glanced behind him and grimaced as he picked up the chair. After a few seconds he sat back down and put his head in his hands.

Patience. Men had to be left to think things through. In a few days Will Carter would probably be claiming the idea was his own. Or maybe not.

He lifted his head slightly, his deep blue eyes locking on hers. 'You really think this could work?'

She nodded slowly. 'I think it's a darn sight better idea than dealing with El Creepo footballer. You know he's a recipe for disaster.'

Will groaned and leaned back in the chair. 'I

know he is. But people like him. Even if he is a prat.'

She smiled at him. 'No, Will. People like *you*.' She let the words hang in the air for a second or two.

He was still looking sceptical. 'Do you honestly think you could persuade my exes to take part?'

She bit her lip. 'If I pitch it right they will be jumping all over this. There's nothing like a woman scorned.'

He grimaced. 'But I never wanted to hurt any of them. And this will just bring all those bad feelings to the surface again.'

'And some of those bad feelings are exactly what we need. Those bad feelings will probably give us some spectacular dares that the public will be willing to pick up the phone and vote for.'

She hated that it sounded so mercenary. It wasn't really Rose's nature but the reality was, if Will really wanted publicity for his charity in a short space of time this was exactly the way to do it.

He started pacing. She could almost see his brain ticking over all the pros and cons.

'I'm still worried. Two of my exes will probably be fine. They've moved on. They've got married. Both of them have told me they were glad things didn't work out between us.' He waved his hand and gave a rueful smile. 'They know we just weren't right for each other. And they've got their happy ever after with someone else.' He frowned. 'Another has got into the media spotlight. The extra publicity will probably suit her. Looking back, I'm sure that's why she dated me in the first place. But the fourth? I just don't know…'

'Is this the one you actually left at the altar?'

He nodded and shook his head. 'Melissa was fiancée number two. I still feel terrible. She didn't take things well and she still hates me.'

'Might this be a little redemption for her? A way to draw a line under things?'

'I just don't know.' He pulled out his phone.

'What are you doing?'

'I'm going to talk to Violet.'

For the weirdest reason her heart plummeted. 'You are?' How ridiculous. Violet was his best friend. Of course he wanted to talk to her. It was only natural.

But it made her stomach curl up in the strangest way.

A way she'd never felt before.

She'd never once been jealous of her sister. They were close. They always supported each other. They'd never had a serious falling-out. Only the usual sisterly spats. But all of a sudden she was feeling strangely jealous of the relationship between Violet and Will. He trusted her. He valued her opinion. And it was almost as if he were second-guessing her advice.

The call lasted only a minute and there was nothing secret about it. She could hear Violet's shrieks of laughter at the other end of the phone. 'It's perfect. The press will love it. I told you my sister was a genius!'

Guilt flooded through her, heat rushing to her cheeks. Violet always had her back, always—even in the worst of circumstances.

Will glanced at her, uncertainty still lacing his eyes. She held her tongue. There was nothing she could say at this point to persuade him. He had to think it through for himself. There was only one natural conclusion he could come to.

She stood up and held out her hand. 'Thank you for a lovely evening, Will. I'm feeling tired. I think I'll go to bed. I take it you've got no ill effects from your headache and I'll be free to go home tomorrow?'

He stared at her outstretched hand for a few seconds. Maybe it was the strange formality between two people who'd kissed a little earlier? But he took a few steps and walked over and shook her hand.

Darn it. There it was again. The little shot straight up her arm, tingling all the way. No matter how many times she tried to ignore it, it wasn't a figment of her imagination. His hand was warm and firm.

It was the first time she'd been around Will and he looked anything less than confident and sure of himself. Her suggestions for publicity had obviously unsettled him.

'Thank you, Rose,' he said distractedly.

She turned away to head back in the house. It was odd. The strangest feeling. She'd much preferred it when the atmosphere between them had been light and flirty. This horrible unsettled feeling was uncomfortable. As much as she didn't want to admit it, being around Will Carter was a lot more interesting than she'd first expected.

Her head told her one thing, and every female hormone in her body told her a whole other. It was exhausting.

But she was curious to see where it would take her.

'Rose?' She turned at the sound of his voice, her heart giving a little leap in her chest.

'Remember Monday—the business conference. We'll find you a caterer.'

'Sure.' She nodded, hoping to not let the disappointment show. 'Thanks.'

She turned back and lengthened her strides back into the house.

Monday had never felt so far away.

CHAPTER FIVE

VIOLET AND ROSE waited impatiently on the chaise longue. Their mother was doing her usual—making them wait. 'Do you have your phone to text Daisy?' Violet asked.

'No pictures,' yelled their mother from the other room. 'I don't want there to be any possibility of a leak to the press.'

The girls rolled their eyes at each other. Sherry had already tried on eleven dresses from various designer friends ranging from barely there to tulle princess. None of them had really suited. 'Has she given you any instructions on the flowers yet?' Rose whispered.

Violet nodded. 'And I'm sworn to secrecy. I've not to say a word.'

'But you can tell me.'

Violet shook her head. 'Not even you.'

Rose felt the indignation rise in her chest. 'You've got to be joking. After everything that's been dumped on me—you're not allowed to tell me about the flowers?'

Violet shrugged. She was entirely used to their mother's little quibbles and obviously didn't think it was worth getting tied in a knot about.

She shot Rose a look. That kind of look. 'So how's things with you and my best friend?'

Rose could feel the hackles rise at the back of her neck. She was instantly on the defensive. 'What do you mean?'

'Have you kissed him yet?'

'What? Why on earth did you ask me that?'

Violet counted off on her fingers. 'Because he's Will Carter. He's charming. He's lovable. And everyone loves him.' She lifted her eyebrows. 'And you two haven't met before. And don't think I didn't notice the little buzz of chemistry yesterday. What's going on?'

Rose was annoyed. 'Chemistry? There was no chemistry. The guy climbed into my bed and I cracked him over the head with a vase. How is that chemistry?'

'But you spent all day yesterday with him *and* you spent the night at his place.'

If only she knew that Rose had spent the whole night tossing and turning in the bed at Gideon Hall wondering—even for a second—if Will might appear. Useless thoughts. Ridiculous thoughts. And thoughts that had made her even angrier and made her feel even more foolish as the dark hours of night had turned into the early hours of morning.

'Nothing happened. Absolutely nothing. You know exactly why I had to stay there—because *you* wouldn't help me.'

Violet gave a few tuts. 'Wow. I think the girl protests too much,' she joked. 'Watch out. He'll sucker you in.'

Rose sucked in a deep breath, ready to erupt at her sister but she didn't get that far.

'What about this one?' Their mother's voice cracked a little as they turned to face her.

Sherry Huntingdon had never lost her model figure or her mane of golden locks. She easily looked fifteen years younger than she actually was.

Rose gasped and lifted her hand to her mouth. 'Oh, Mum, that's it. That's the one. It's perfect.'

Violet was on her feet, walking over to touch the ruched fabric scattered with tiny jewels. The dress was a showstopper. It hugged every curve of her frame, fitting like a glove in satin covered in tiny sparkling jewels with a huge fishtail.

'You think?' Yes, her voice was definitely breaking. It was all getting too much for her. It was the perfect dress for the perfect wedding.

'I love it, Mum,' said Rose with pride. Her

mother had never looked quite so stunning as she did today.

'Veil or no veil?'

'No veil.' Both girls spoke in unison, then turned to each other and laughed.

Their mum hesitated a second. 'I've picked a dress for all three of you. You just need to pick a colour each.' She held up a bright blue dress on a hanger. It had sheer shoulders, a fitted bodice with a jewel clasp gathered just under the breasts and a loose full-length skirt. 'Do you think it will suit Daisy? I didn't want to pick something that made her pregnancy so obvious.'

Rose nodded. 'I think it looks great.' She held the layers of material in the skirt and swished it from side to side. 'What colour do you want, Violet?'

'Either red or dark purple. What about you?'

'I like this bright blue. Will we wear jewel colours? Do you think Daisy would wear emerald green?'

'I don't see why not.' She nodded. 'Bright colours would be nice.' Violet exchanged a glance with her mother. It was obvious thoughts were spinning through her brain. Rose was curious. What were they thinking about?

'We'll talk colours later,' Sherry said quickly before spinning around. 'Now, will someone unzip me so we can talk headpieces?'

* * *

Rose was exhausted. Her mother's dress was picked. Their dresses were more or less agreed on, and they'd tried on an endless amount of jewellery and headpieces yesterday. And that was only the dresses.

She'd emailed a number of caterers and not had one single response. Marquee companies were being equally silent and it was all starting to make her panic. Hopefully things would be better with Will today.

He'd assured her that as long as they were willing to pay a premium price they'd be able to find someone suitable.

She shifted nervously on her feet and fiddled with an earring while she waited for him to arrive. Two minutes later she could hear the purr of a car coming down the driveway. Will pulled up in a car identical to her father's vintage Rolls-Royce only this time in silver. She raised her eyebrows in surprise as he climbed out and walked around to open her door for her.

'What?' He grinned. 'Did you think only your dad had one of these?'

She climbed in. 'I thought you would have wanted something more modern—more environmentally friendly.' It was a nice touch—a man opening a door for her.

He slid into the seat next to her. 'Quality and

class. I spent a number of years waiting to buy this car. Now I've got it, I fully intend to drive it.'

She squinted at the row of stitches on his head. The swelling had definitely gone down now and she could see the edges pulled tightly together. 'How's your head? Does it hurt?'

'Is that concern after what—two days?' He was mocking her, trying to get a rise out of her. He leaned a little closer conspiratorially. 'It's itchy. I thought I was going to have to put a set of gloves on last night to stop me scratching it in my sleep.'

'Ouch. Isn't there a cream or something you can put on it to stop it itching?'

He shook his head as the car sped along the winding country roads and headed towards the motorway. 'I'm not to touch it at all. So scratching is definitely not allowed!'

There it was again. That annoying little flutter in her stomach that let her know this was her fault.

'Do you really think we'll find a caterer today? I'm getting worried. I've contacted a few and heard nothing.'

He nodded as they turned towards the motorway. 'I think we'll find someone. I hope you're hungry.'

'Why?'

'Because they'll all have workstations and

they'll be cooking so all the businesses can sample their food. Catering an event is a really big deal. It pays big bucks. They go all out at these events.'

'Really? We'll get to eat the food?'

He smiled. 'Really. I guarantee you. You won't be able to eat for a week after this.'

She sighed and leaned back into the comfortable leather seat as they started to hit the traffic. 'It's just a pity we can't clone Judy and get her to make all the food. That chicken the other night was great.'

He smiled in appreciation. 'She's great. And no. You can't have her. She's my secret weapon.'

She shuffled in the seat. 'Have you given any more thought to the publicity?' Great. She could see his knuckles tighten on the steering wheel and start to blanch.

'Let's talk about it later.' He leaned over and turned on the radio. The conversation was obviously over. Rose turned and looked out of the window. She was still ticking off things in her head. She'd have to talk to Will about marquees; they were proving a real problem. If she could get the caterer sorted out today that would be at least one more thing off her list. Then it would be into the murky world of wedding favours and table decorations.

Will signalled and pulled off the motorway towards the conference centre. The car park was already jam-packed but he moved straight to the valet parking at the front and jumped out. Rose didn't even want to consider how much this was costing.

The conference centre was full of people in designer-cut suits and Italian leather shoes. She looked down at her simple fitted beige trousers and white loose shirt with a variety of beads. 'You should have warned me I'm underdressed,' she hissed. 'I could have changed.'

His brow wrinkled as he walked forward. 'You look perfect. What are you worrying about?' He glanced at the map in his hands. 'Here, Hall C is where all the caterers are. Let's head there.'

He nodded and said hello to a few folk as they wove their way through the crowds. There really wasn't much need for the map. The smells emanating from Hall C would have led them in the right direction.

It was definitely the busiest part. Will didn't hesitate. He made his way straight over to the first booth and picked up a disposable plate and fork. 'Come on,' he whispered. 'Have a quick taste. If you don't like it we'll move on.'

The aroma of spicy chicken and beef was wafting around her, making her ravenous. She took a spoonful and grabbed a taste just as Will did.

Her eyes watered and she turned to face him, trying not to laugh.

Within a few seconds he had a similar expression on his face. He gestured towards a nearby table stocked with iced water and glasses. 'Water?' The word squeaked out and she had to put a hand in front of her mouth. She nodded and followed quickly to the table, grabbing the glass of iced water that he poured. She swallowed swiftly and allowed the cool water to ease her scorching throat. 'Wow. I think they overdid the chillies.' She could almost feel a tear in her eye.

Will gulped down a second glass of water. 'Well, that was a wake-up call.' He grabbed her hand. 'Here, let's go somewhere things will be more soothing.'

He pulled her over towards an Italian stand where lasagne, spaghetti bolognaise and chicken *arrabiata* were all waiting to be sampled. They both played safe, taking a small sample of lasagne and spaghetti. It was good. Meaty, creamy with just the right amount of herbs. 'It's lovely,' Rose sighed. 'But it wouldn't do for Mum and Dad's wedding.'

Will nodded. 'Let's try some more.' Half an hour later they'd tried some Chinese food, some sushi, some Indian food and lots of traditional English dishes. Rose was no closer to finding something she really liked. She was pushing some food around her plate. 'Oh, no. This chicken looks a bit pink. I'm not eating that.'

Will whipped the plate out of her hand and dumped it in the rubbish bin. 'Wait. There's someone I know. His food is good. Let's try him.'

He walked with confidence, his hand encircling hers just as it had all day. It sent nice little impulses up her arm and gave her a strange sense of belonging. England had always been her home. She'd lived at Huntingdon Hall since she'd been a little girl. But spending most of her time in New York these last three years had given her a bit of space and distance.

Being around Will was making her think hard about her choices. Her father had already mentioned she would need to be back here for the band's European tour. But as much as she loved New York and her friends, it was beginning to lose its shine. Seeing her younger sister Daisy get married had made her feel a little flutter of homesickness. Knowing that Daisy would have a baby soon and wanting to be around her new niece or nephew definitely made her want to stay close to home.

Will steered her over towards a new stand. 'Hi, Frank. This is my friend Rose Huntingdon-Cross. We're hoping to get an event catered soon.'

Frank put his hand out and shook Rose's hand warmly. 'Pleasure to meet you. Tell me what you

YOUR PARTICIPATION IS REQUESTED!

Dear Reader,

Since you are a lover of our books – we would like to get to know you!

Inside you will find a short Reader's Survey. Sharing your answers with us will help our editorial staff understand who you are and what activities you enjoy.

To thank you for your participation, we would like to send you 2 books and 2 gifts – **ABSOLUTELY FREE!**

Enjoy your gifts with our appreciation,

Pam Powers

**SEE INSIDE
FOR READER'S
SURVEY**

For Your Reading Pleasure...

We'll send you 2 books and 2 gifts
ABSOLUTELY FREE
just for completing our Reader's Survey!

YOURS FREE!
We'll send you two fabulous surprise gifts absolutely FREE, just for trying our books!

YOUR READER'S SURVEY
"THANK YOU" FREE GIFTS INCLUDE:
- ▶ 2 FREE books
- ▶ 2 lovely surprise gifts

PLEASE FILL IN THE CIRCLES COMPLETELY TO RESPOND

1) What type of fiction books do you enjoy reading? (Check all that apply)
- ○ Suspense/Thrillers
- ○ Action/Adventure
- ○ Modern-day Romances
- ○ Historical Romance
- ○ Humour
- ○ Paranormal Romance

2) What attracted you most to the last fiction book you purchased on impulse?
- ○ The Title
- ○ The Cover
- ○ The Author
- ○ The Story

3) What is usually the greatest influencer when you <u>plan</u> to buy a book?
- ○ Advertising
- ○ Referral
- ○ Book Review

4) How often do you access the internet?
- ○ Daily
- ○ Weekly
- ○ Monthly
- ○ Rarely or never.

5) How many NEW paperback fiction novels have you purchased in the past 3 months?
- ○ 0 - 2
- ○ 3 - 6
- ○ 7 or more

YES! I have completed the Reader's Survey. Please send me the 2 FREE books and 2 FREE gifts (gifts are worth about $10) for which I qualify. I understand that I am under no obligation to purchase any books, as explained on the back of this card.

119/319 HDL GH3M

FIRST NAME	LAST NAME

ADDRESS

APT.#	CITY

STATE/PROV.   ZIP/POSTAL CODE

HARLEQUIN READER SERVICE —Here's How It Works:

Accepting your 2 free Harlequin® Romance Larger Print books and 2 free gifts (gifts valued at approximately $10.00) places you under no obligation to buy anything. You may keep the books and gifts and return the shipping statement marked "cancel." If you do not cancel, about a month later we'll send you 4 additional books and bill you just $5.09 each in the U.S. or $5.49 each in Canada. That is a savings of at least 15% off the cover price. It's quite a bargain! Shipping and handling is just 50¢ per book in the U.S. and 75¢ per book in Canada.* You may cancel at any time, but if you choose to continue, every month we'll send you 4 more books, which you may either purchase at the discount price or return to us and cancel your subscription. *Terms and prices subject to change without notice. Prices do not include applicable taxes. Sales tax applicable in N.Y. Canadian residents will be charged applicable taxes. Offer not valid in Quebec. Books received may not be as shown. All orders subject to credit approval. Credit or debit balances in a customer's account(s) may be offset by any other outstanding balance owed by or to the customer. Please allow 4 to 6 weeks for delivery. Offer available while quantities last.

want to taste. Any friend of Will's is a friend of mine.'

Rose smiled. The first stall that seemed promising. 'My parents' tastes are simple. My mother likes chicken. My father steak. They just like them to taste exquisite. What you do with them is up to you.'

'Chicken and steak. My two favourite English dishes. Give me a second.'

He knelt behind the counter and put up a range of plates. 'Okay, steak. Here's a plain sirloin. I can give you gravy, pepper sauce or whisky and mushroom sauce. Here's my version of steak stroganoff, and another steak traditional stew. For chicken I have chicken with cider, apples, mushroom and cream, a chicken stew with tomatoes and pepper and a traditional Balmoral chicken with haggis and pepper sauce.'

The plates appeared one after another with a variety of cutlery. Will smiled broadly. This guy could be perfect. As Rose worked her way along the row each dish tasted every bit as good as the one before. She sighed as she reached the end.

Frank was standing with his arms crossed. 'What's your dessert wish list?'

She turned to face Will, who was finishing off the sirloin steak with some mushroom sauce. 'Really? You knew this guy and didn't phone him straight away?'

Will smiled. 'He's my secret weapon. Everyone's tastes are different. Frank's always my number one choice.'

She looked up at Frank. 'Dessert would be something chocolate and orange for my mother and something strawberry or raspberry for my father.'

'No problem.' He disappeared again and started thumping plates up onto the deck. 'Chocolate and orange torte, raspberry pavlova, strawberry cheesecake, chocolate and cherry gateau and chocolate and raspberry roulade.'

Rose felt her eyes widen. 'I've just died and gone to heaven.' She lifted a fork and worked her way along the dishes, reaching the end as her taste buds exploded. 'All of them. I want all of them.'

Frank's smile reached from one ear to the other. He pulled out a diary. 'When's your event? Next year? Two years away?'

Rose gulped and glanced at Will for help. 'Eh, just under four weeks.'

'What?' Frank's voice echoed around the surrounding area.

Will moved swiftly behind the counter, putting his arm around Frank's shoulders. 'This is a very big event, Frank. And if I tell you money is no object, would it help?' He pointed towards Rose. 'Her mum and dad are renewing their wedding vows. They have a massive kitchen that you will be able to have full run of. You might have heard of them: rock star Rick Cross and ex-model Sherry Huntingdon. It's pretty much going to be the celebrity wedding renewal of the year. Everyone will be talking about who catered it.'

Frank's face had initially paled but as Will kept talking she could see the pieces falling into place in his brain. 'I have reservations for the next two years. Taking something on like this would be no mean feat. I'd have to hire other staff and make alternative arrangements for my other booking without scrimping on quality.'

Rose's stomach was currently tied up in knots. His food was perfect. His food was *better* than perfect and would suit her mum and dad and their exacting needs far more than anything else she'd seen today.

'Please, Frank. Can you have a look at your diary and see if you can make this work? Your food is fantastic. Mum and Dad would love your menu.'

He hesitated as he flicked through an appointment book in front of him. 'That date is for a corporate event—not another wedding. I'd be able to let my second-in-command take charge. But I'd need extra staff.' He stared off into the distance as if his brain was mulling things over.

'I'd also need to see the kitchen before I make a final decision.'

Rose found herself nodding automatically. She was sure the kitchen would meet his standards and if there was anything else he needed—she'd find it. 'Any time, Frank. Any time you want to see the kitchens would be fine with me. Just say the word.'

He glanced between Will and Rose once again. 'This will be expensive. You realise that, don't you?'

Rose answered quickly as she pulled out one of her business cards and handed it to him. 'I've tasted your food. You're worth it. Don't worry about the costs. Do you need a deposit?' She pulled out the corporate credit card she usually used for all the band expenses. It had the biggest credit limit.

He waggled his finger. 'I haven't seen the kitchen yet.' Then he laughed and turned to Will. 'Where did you find this one? She's your best yet—by an absolute mile.'

Rose felt her cheeks flush with colour. 'No, I mean…we're not… There's nothing going on between us.'

Frank winked. 'That's what they all say.'

Will tried to break the awkwardness, but his immediate reaction was to slide his arm around her shoulders and pull her closer. 'Rose and I are just good friends. I'm helping her out with the wedding stuff for her parents and she's helping me out with some publicity for the homeless charity.'

Frank looked at her again. This time she could see a flicker of respect behind his glance. He held out his fist towards Will's and they bumped them together. 'See you Wednesday night at the soup kitchen?' He waved the card. 'I'll call you later today and arrange to come and see the kitchens, okay?'

'Absolutely. That's great. Thanks very much.'

Will steered her away and over towards an ice-cream stand. The warmth from his arm was seeping through her shoulders. She should object to him holding her so closely—particularly when there was no reason. But something felt right about this. It was almost as if she were a good fit.

She gave him a nudge. 'I forgot to tell you. There's a wedding fair on Saturday in one of the nearby hotels. Will you come with me to try and sort out some of the other arrangements?'

He groaned. 'I can't think of anything worse. I hate wedding fairs with a passion. I've been at more than I could count.'

She grinned. 'Good. Then it won't be a problem. I'll come for you at ten o'clock.'

He raised his eyebrows. 'You'll come for me?'

She nodded. 'I'll try and drive something inconspicuous. The sooner we get in, the sooner we get out.'

'Okay, I can live with that.'

'You never told me you volunteered at the shelter, too.'

He looked down at her. 'Didn't I? I just thought you would know. Violet's come along a few times to help when numbers have been short. I go there once a week. It helps me try and connect with the people I'm trying to help. Some of their stories would break your heart.' He stopped walking and turned her to face him, placing his hands on her shoulders. 'I'm completely serious about this.'

'I know that. I get that.' She could see the worry and concern on his face.

'That's why I'm so hesitant to do what you suggested. I get that it's a good idea. But I don't want this to be about me. I want it to be about *them*.'

She lifted her hand up to his arm and gave it a squeeze. 'I understand. I really do. But our world doesn't always work the way we want it to, Will. If it did—none of those people would be homeless in the first place. I can't give you a long-term fix here. What I can give you is a way to get people talking about the charity—because that will happen. But first, we need an angle.'

He sighed. 'And the angle is me.'

The guy standing in front of her now wasn't the Runaway Groom. He wasn't a guy that had made a host of headlines in all the tabloids. He was sincere. He was committed to his charity. And he wanted to do the best he could for it. There was a whole other side to Will Carter that no one else knew about. If she'd thought he was charming before, she hadn't counted on how much a little glimpse into the real Will could actually impact on her heart.

She nodded. 'Are you worried about the trials your exes might suggest?'

He shook his head and gave a rueful smile. 'I probably should be, but that's actually the last thing I'm worried about.' He reached over and tucked a wayward lock of blonde hair behind her ear. It was the simplest movement.

But the feel of his finger against her cheek sent her back to the church on the island. Back to the feel of his lips on hers. Back to the surge of hormones that had swept her body and done crazy things to her brain.

If she stood on her tiptoes right now their noses would brush together and their lips could touch again.

She needed a reality check soon.

And there was only one way to get it.

She gave his arm another squeeze. 'Then let's get this done. You need to give me details on who they are—and how to contact them. Leave it to me. I can deal with them.'

There. Nothing like a bucket of cold water over the two of them to break the mood.

His arms dropped from her shoulders. 'Sure. Let's see what I can do.'

He walked away in front of her, heading towards the exit. She waited a second. Letting her heart rate come back to normal and trying not to fixate on his backside.

Her stomach gave a little flutter. Nothing like hearing about all Will's bad points from his multitude of fiancées to give her a little perspective.

CHAPTER SIX

WILL WOKE UP with his head thumping. A wedding fair was the last thing he needed. Helium balloons and tiny bottles of whisky were not filling him with joy.

He threw on his running gear and went for a run in the grounds, circling the house and gardens a few times, then pounding around the lake. Running was always therapeutic for Will. It helped him clear away the cobwebs and get some clarity on things.

But the cobwebs this morning were Rose shaped. And they didn't plan on moving no matter what he did.

The last thing he wanted to do was let her down. So, no matter how much he hated it, he would spend the day talking about wedding favours, chair covers and balloons.

Everything about this should be making him run for the hills. But the promise of being around Rose again was just far too enticing. He pounded harder on the driveway. No matter how hard he tried, Rose Huntingdon-Cross was finding a way under his skin. It didn't matter the messages that his brain was sending. The messages from his body were a whole other matter. And they were definitely leading the charge.

He rounded back to the main front door just as his phone beeped. A text. From Violet.

What you doing today?

His stomach dropped with a surge of guilt. He texted quickly before he changed his mind.

Helping Rose with wedding arrangements.

He waited. Expecting Violet to send something back. But she didn't. And it made him feel even worse. It had only been a few days but he was neglecting her. Any day she'd call him on it and ask him what was going on.

Then he'd be in trouble.

He strode through the hallway and up the stairs, hitting the shower in his room. He automatically pulled a suit from his cupboard, then stared at it, and put it back. This wasn't a suit kind of day. Hell, the last thing he wanted was to be mistaken for a groom.

He pulled on a short-sleeved shirt and a pair of

army trousers before driving to the local surgery and getting the nurse to remove his stitches. The scar was still angry and red but she assured him it would fade over time and he arrived back just as Rose was pulling up outside the house. She gave him a hard stare as he climbed into the tiny Mini.

'You got your stitches out?'

He nodded. 'It's official. I'm now Harry Potter and I'll get all the girls.' He looked around. 'What's up?' She had her black planner sitting on her lap.

Rose was perfect as always. She was wearing a pink and white fifties-style dress. It was demure and gave nothing away. But he'd already seen and touched what lay beneath those clothes. His fingers started to tingle.

'Is this the casual look?' she asked stiffly.

'What—you wanted me to wear a suit and pretend to be a groom? You think I haven't had enough practice at that?'

She frowned. 'Well, it could have been part of our disguise. I'm not sure I want to tell people today that I'm organising a wedding renewal for my parents. The news isn't exactly out yet.'

'Haven't you contacted their friends with the date?'

He didn't want to appear critical. But he could only imagine that most of Rick and Sherry's guest list would already have bulging diaries.

Rose was concentrating on the road. She was cute when she was driving, glasses perched at the end of her nose.

'I have. But there's always a few I can't get hold of.' She rolled her eyes without diverting them from the road. 'And you know, they're the ones that have a monster-size tantrum if they hear the news from anyone else.'

'Tell them to get over it.'

'What?' She seemed shocked by his abrupt tone.

'These people are adults. If they want information they should check their emails or answering machines. I hate the way some of these celebrities want to be spoon-fed. They act like a bunch of toddlers.'

He heard her suck in a breath as if she were thinking what to say. Had he just offended her? Violet was so normal he just assumed that Sherry and Rick didn't behave like other celebrities. Rose was biting her lip.

He couldn't help himself. He couldn't wait. 'Are you mad?'

She shook her head. 'No. I'm not mad. And I guess you're right. It's just I get used to dealing with these kinds of people.' She wrinkled her nose. 'And it starts to all seem normal to me instead of outrageous.'

She turned the car towards a country estate.

The road was already backed up with cars and Will sank lower in his seat. 'I've got a bad feeling about this.'

She laughed and gave him a slap. 'Oh, come on. How bad can it be?'

'You've never met a bunch of Bridezillas, have you?'

She pulled over. The car park was jammed and the traffic was virtually at a standstill.

'You're parking here? On the driveway?'

She nodded and smiled. 'Why not? In the next five minutes everyone else will, too. Let's go.'

She climbed out into the morning sun and waited for Will to join her. Everywhere they looked there were people. The doorway was crowded, so they walked around the large mansion house and went in another entrance at the back. Will pulled out some cash to pay their entrance fee and picked up a leaflet with a floor plan.

Rose had an amused smile on her face. 'These things have a floor plan?'

He laughed and put an arm around her shoulders. 'Let me introduce you to the world of crazy brides. If we hang out here all day I guarantee at some point we'll see two brides scrapping over a date somewhere.'

'No way.'

He nodded solemnly. 'Way.' He glanced at the plan. 'What first?'

She screwed up her nose and leaned against him, her scent reaching up around him. It was light and floral, like a summer day. Just exactly the way a girl called Rose should smell. 'We don't need to wait for the fashion show of the bridal dresses. That's all sorted. Let's hit the favours. I'm still not really sure what we should get.'

Will guided her through the large mansion rooms. 'Lots of people just go for the traditional—miniature bottles of whisky for guys and some kind of trinket or chocolates for the women. Lottery tickets are popular, too.'

Rose shook her head. 'I don't think my mother would be happy if I gave her wedding guests a lottery ticket. It has to be something more personal than that.'

'More personal for around two hundred people?'

He could see her bite the inside of her cheek. 'More like three hundred.'

The room was already crowded and they walked around. Some things were cute. Some things were practical. And some things were just quirky.

Rose held up flip-flops in different colours. 'What are these for?'

The girl behind the counter smiled. 'It's our

most popular item right now. Flip-flops for the women who've been wearing their stiletto heels all day and want to spend the night dancing.'

Rose nodded. 'Good idea.' She moved on to the next stall, which had personalised notebooks with pictures of the bride and the groom on the front. Little heart-shaped glass pendants. Handkerchiefs with the bride and groom's name and date of wedding stitched on them.

He could see her visibly wince at some of the more cringeworthy items. She turned and sighed. 'I don't see anything I love.'

Will breathed in deeply and caught the whiff of something sweet. In the far corner there was a glass counter from one of the most well-known stores in London. 'How about chocolates?'

She walked over next to him. 'Isn't that a little boring? A few chocolates in an individual box for the guests?'

'How about you try and personalise it? Strawberry, orange, blackcurrant, limes—you could find out people's favourites. In fact,' he bent forward and whispered in her ear, 'if you speak very nicely to that man behind the counter and showed him your guest list I bet you he already knows some of the favourites of the people on it.'

Will bent over and picked up a triangular bag of popcorn. 'Some of the guys might prefer this. They've got shortbread, too. They even do mini-doughnuts.' He shrugged. 'Everybody eats. Everybody likes food. If you personalise it as much as you can it could be a hit.'

She was beginning to look a little more relaxed. The room was starting to get crowded. She shot him a smile. 'Give me five minutes to see what I can do.'

She disappeared across the room in a flash and within two minutes was behind the counter charming the white-gloved chocolatier. She pulled out a list and the two conferred over it for a few minutes before the chocolatier carefully folded it and put it in his pocket. Rose pulled out her chequebook and quickly scribbled a cheque, leaving her card.

She came rushing back over with a small basket of chocolate creams in her hand.

'Success?'

She was beaming. 'Better than success. He's even going to come to the wedding and set up the counter for the day.'

'As well as do all the favours?'

She picked up a chocolate and popped it in her mouth. 'Mmm...strawberry, delicious.' She held out the basket. 'Do you want one?'

'I'm not sure—is it safe? If I didn't know any better I'd say you were guarding them with your life.' He was laughing. Even though she'd offered a chocolate she'd automatically pulled the basket back to her chest as if she were daring anyone to try and take one.

She looked down at the basket and reluctantly pushed it forward again. He waved his hand. 'Forget it. I know when there's a line in the sand.' He leaned forward. 'Are you going to tell me how much all this is going to cost?'

Rose smiled and popped another chocolate in her mouth. 'Absolutely not. Now, let's look over here. The chocolatier just gave me the best idea in the world.'

They walked towards a smaller stand at the back of the hall. It was covered in jewellery and different mementos, a lot of them encrusted in crystals. She picked up the nearest one and shot the guy behind the table her biggest smile.

'I think you're about to hate me, but Paul, the chocolatier, sent me over.'

The guy smiled and rolled his eyes as Rose let out a gasp and picked up a little jewelled guitar. 'Oh, this is it. This is so perfect.' She spun to face Will. 'How perfect is it? A jewelled guitar for Rick and Sherry's wedding renewal?' She could feel the excitement building in her chest. Trouble was, the workmanship of the guitar set with jewelled stones was beautiful. How long did it take to make?

She took a deep breath. 'What would you say

if I asked for three hundred of these in three weeks' time?'

The guy's jaw bounced off the floor. 'I'd say, "Do you know how much that would cost?"'

She nodded. 'I think I have a pretty good idea.'

He held out his hand towards her and walked around the table. 'John Taylor.' He wrinkled his nose. 'Rick and Sherry? Are you talking about Rick Cross?'

She nodded. 'He's my father. My parents are renewing their vows. I'd really love it if we could have some of the mini-jewelled guitars as favours.'

She could see him bite his lip. 'I'm a huge fan.' He sighed. 'The guitars are ready. The stones just need to be glued in place. They're semi-precious crystals. It takes a bit of time. But...' he paused '...for Rick Cross? I think I could pull out all the stops.'

'You could?' Rose let out a squeal and flung her arms around the guy. Will's face creased into a frown but she was too busy pulling out her credit card and setting up the order to pay too much attention.

After a few minutes she glanced around, placing her hand on Will's arm. 'Now help me find, accost and probably blackmail some company into hiring me a marquee for the day.'

He rolled his eyes. 'You'll need an even bigger chequebook for that.'

But Rose was getting lost in the atmosphere of the place. 'I think I want ones that have those fairy lights at night—you know, so it looks all magical?'

Her hair tickled his nose as he bent forward. 'Watch out, you're in danger of turning into one of the Bridezillas. I think you've been bitten by the bug.'

She stopped walking abruptly and turned around. 'Oh, no. Don't be fooled. Not for a second. This is my mother's dream wedding. Not mine.'

'And it was pretty much Daisy's, too.'

She nodded. 'I know. But I don't want any of this.'

He wasn't convinced—not for a second. 'Doesn't every girl want a dream wedding and to feel like a princess on the day they marry?'

But Rose's face was deadly serious. 'Absolutely not. Seeing all the chaos with Daisy getting married just made me even more convinced. The only part of that wedding that mattered was the two people standing at the front and looking at each other as if they couldn't wait to say they'd love each other for ever.' A Bridezilla pushed her from behind as she hurried past, and Rose almost face-planted into his chest.

He pulled her close and put a protective arm around her waist. She sighed. 'I definitely don't want all this. I want me and my Mr For Ever alone—just the two of us—saying our vows without any of the kerfuffle.'

He smiled at her choice of word. 'Kerfuffle? I don't think I've heard that in years.'

She raised her hands to the bedlam around them and lifted her head towards his. 'Well, isn't that the most accurate description? Who needs it? Not me.'

Something soothing and warm was washing over him. Four fiancées. And not one of them had ever wanted this. He'd known all along how different Rose was. He'd known she was sneaking under his defences in every which way. He just hadn't realised how much. And it was the way she'd said those words. *Me and my Mr For Ever alone*. The words *Mr For Ever* should have terrified him. But for the first time in his life they didn't.

'Really? You really don't want all this?' He knew she'd loved the church on the island and remarked how perfect it was. But he hadn't been entirely sure that wasn't just saying she didn't want a big wedding. But the one thing Rose couldn't hide was the sincerity in her eyes. His head was crammed full of thoughts of the palavers over wedding plans with the four previous fiancées. Not one of them would have agreed to walk away from the dream and just have the husband.

Today was totally different. Today he didn't want to run from the room in the start of a mild panic. That could be easily explained. This wasn't his wedding and Rose wasn't his fiancée. But everything about this felt different. And it felt different because of Rose.

Her face was just inches from his. Her pale blue eyes unblinking. 'I really don't want any of this,' she whispered.

The buzz around him was fading away. All he could concentrate on was the face in front of him. All similarities to her sister had vanished in the mist. This was Rose. This was only Rose. The woman who was having more of an effect on him than he could even begin to comprehend.

Any minute now a white charger would appear in the room and he'd just pick her up and sweep her off somewhere.

But being Rose, she would probably object.

She lifted a hand up and placed it on his chest. The warmth from her palm flooded through his fine shirt and their gazes locked and held for a second.

Was she really having the same kind of thoughts that he was?

Then it happened. A wayward thought he

could never have dreamed of. He could actually imagine doing all this kind of stuff with Rose.

Was it because her vision of a wedding was close to his? Because the funny thing was, even if she changed her mind, he could see himself doing all this planning with Rose. Rose felt right. Rose felt like a part of him.

For Will it was like a revelation. Fireworks were going off in his head. His brain was spinning and his mouth resembled the Sahara desert. Was this it? Was this what it felt like for other people? Was this what it felt like for Rick and Sherry?

Her eyes twinkled and a grin appeared on her face. 'Come on, wedding guy. There were three things on the list today. Favours—done. But you promised me marquees and balloons—you better deliver.'

The spark in her eyes broke the increasing tension between them and brought him back to reality. He had to be sure. He had to be *more* than sure. The last thing he wanted to do was hurt Rose.

He nodded and grabbed her hand. 'Let's see how quickly we can do this. There's a bridal show about to start. Everyone will disappear to watch that.' All he really wanted to do was get out of here and get Rose all to himself.

It didn't take long. It just took an exceptional

amount of money. But they finally found someone who could supply a marquee—complete with
twinkling fairy lights—on the date they needed.
Once they heard the magic words *Rick Cross and
Sherry Huntingdon* the deal was done.

The balloons were another matter. One side
of the hall had a whole range of displays and
colours, from table decorations with a few helium balloons to archways covering the whole
top table.

'Do you know what colour scheme your mum
will want?'

'Yep, jewel colours. Bright and bold. Red,
green and blue.' She wandered between all the
stands touching all the metallic bobbing balloons,
some held down by balloon weights and some
tied to walls and chair backs.

'What's the story?' he asked. 'Were you the
kid that never got bought a balloon?'

She smiled and tipped her head to the side. 'I
just like them, that's all. Don't get me wrong—if
you ever tried to get me in a big balloon—up in
the sky—I'd run in the opposite direction. But
these…' she jiggled her hand amongst an array
of bobbing balloons '…I just love.' She pointed
ahead. 'See those ones, all heart-shaped and just
the colours I need? I'd love a really big display
like that in all four corners of the marquees.'

Will stared at the bobbing balloons. They made

him nauseous. He couldn't understand the attraction. The heat in the mansion house was starting to rise. The number of people surrounding them seemed to be growing and growing. He couldn't wait to get out of there. He had a one-track mind—get Rose away from all these people and just to himself.

The double doors in the large room they were in opened out onto the wide gardens. But the air was hardly circulating around them.

Rose took a few moments to place her order and pay by cheque. She walked over smiling. 'I love those. I think they'll be perfect.'

'Good. Can we get out of here now?'

She pivoted on her heels, her dress bouncing out around her. He could see several eyes in the room on her. She really didn't have any idea just how pretty she was, or what a statement her older-style dress made. It was like having Doris Day in the room with them. He couldn't help the smile that spread from one ear to the other.

It was official. This was the Rose effect.

'What about cakes? We haven't looked at cakes yet…' Her voice drifted off as her hand trailed against silver and pink heart balloons in a wide arch next to her.

The bridal show must have just finished as people started to surge through the entrance towards them. Rose stumbled on her square-heeled shoes and fell into the display balloons, dislodging them and making them drift free from their anchor and rise up all around her.

For an instant the whole room held its breath as two hundred balloons escaped their tethers and started floating and bobbing free. Will could see the horror on her face and grabbed her hand as he stifled a laugh and pulled her towards one of the open garden doors.

It was infectious. Rose started laughing too as they burst from the doors, out into the grounds as several balloons escaped around them.

Behind them there were squeals and bedlam. But Will couldn't have cared less. The fresh air of freedom was just too much as they ran across the grass together to where the cars were parked.

The last thing he saw was a pink and silver balloon floating in front of them as they dashed to the car.

CHAPTER SEVEN

ROSE WAITED NERVOUSLY as the phone rang. She was regretting her suggestion big time right now. 'Hello?'

The voice was sharp at the end of the phone.

'Hi, there. This is Rose Huntingdon-Cross. I'm looking for Melissa Kirkwood.'

'Violet's sister? What on earth do you want?'

She cringed at the instant recognition. Melissa was the bride who had been jilted at the altar. She was always going to be the most difficult.

'I'm phoning you because I'm doing some charity work for Will Carter and his homeless charity.'

There was a hiss at the end of the phone. 'Don't even say his name to me!'

It came out with such venom that she was actually taken aback. Although her brain was telling her to stay calm, her tongue just went into overdrive. 'I'm sorry to upset you. It's just—I thought you might be interested in this. We're contacting all of Will Carter's ex-fiancées to see if they would be willing to participate in a charity event. All you'd be required to do is put forward some kind of trial or dare that you'd like Will to do, and it will go to a public vote with all proceeds going to the charity.' Her mouth was gaining momentum like a steam train. 'You can be as horrible as you like with the dare or trial. Pick something you know he would hate to do.'

Oh, no. Had she actually just said that out loud? It was too late. Her PR head had gone into salvage mode. She couldn't take it back now.

There was silence at the end of the phone and a deep intake of breath. Rose's heart thudded in her chest. Part of her wanted Melissa to refuse, the other needed her to say yes. 'We've already negotiated a deal and coverage with the national press—and there will be television interviews, too. So you'll be able to show the world how you've moved on.'

Please let her have moved on, prayed Rose. Will had described some of his exes as a little fame hungry and eager to be in the spotlight. Hopefully the temptation would be too much.

'Just how hideous can I make his dare?' The voice had developed a calculating edge.

'As hideous as you like. At the end of the week's voting he will have to carry out the one with the most public votes.'

She could almost hear Melissa's brain ticking at the end of the phone. 'I need a day to think of something suitable.'

'Absolutely no problem at all. How about I call you back on Tuesday and set up an interview with the press for you then, too?'

Best to kill two birds with one stone. She really didn't want to have prolonged conversations with any of Will's exes. No matter how curious she was about the collection of women. Once she'd made the initial phone calls she was backing out of the limelight and letting the momentum carry the whole thing forward. The newspaper editor had loved it, and one of her favourite morning TV presenters had already agreed to interview all the women on TV.

The tone in Melissa's voice had changed. It was almost as if her brain was currently contemplating exactly what she could plot. 'Tuesday will be fine.' The phone went down with a click and Rose gulped.

She made a mark on the list in front of her. One down. Three to go.

'Rose? Rose, are you there?'

Will's voice echoed down the corridor and his head appeared around the corner of her bedroom door. He was clutching something in his hand and looking a little wary.

By the time she'd finished the phone calls she was exhausted and had adopted the starfish position on her bed. She hadn't moved for the last twenty minutes and didn't have any intention of moving any time soon.

She turned her head. 'If you ever get engaged to a crazy woman again you and I are never talking.'

He winced. 'You've done it? You've called them all?'

He didn't wait to be invited in. He just crossed her room in long strides and sat down at the edge of her bed.

Her head flopped back. 'I've called them all and you owe me—*big time.*' She turned on her side and rested her head on her hand. 'Where on earth did you find them?'

He frowned. 'Don't be like that. All of them have good points. I'm just not their favourite person.'

Rose laughed. 'Oh, you can say that again. Just wait till we find out what the trials are on Tuesday. I have the feeling that some of these ladies will spend the next two days plotting.'

He rolled his eyes. 'Not some. Just one of them.' His fingers drifted over and touched the edge of her trousers. 'I didn't mean to hurt any of them. Things just got out of hand.'

Rose pushed herself up the bed. 'Once or twice

I might let you off with. But four times. Do you never learn your lesson?'

'Looks like I'm about to.' There was something about the way he said the words. He was pretending to be flippant. But the atmosphere had changed quickly around them. She might be relaxed around Will, but it didn't deplete the buzz of electricity she felt whenever he walked in the same room as her.

She sighed. 'What's that?' She pointed to the curled-up newspaper in his hand and flopped back onto the bed.

'Yeah, about that.' Will flopped back onto the bed next to her.

The corners of her lips turned upwards. 'We've been in this position before.'

He smiled, too. 'I know. I remember. I even have the scar to prove it. I'm just hoping I'm not about to earn another one.'

She wrinkled her brow. 'Why would you do that?' It was disconcerting having those dark blue eyes just inches from hers. This was exactly what waking up next to Will Carter would feel like. All six feet four of him just inches away. That rogue thought was doing strange things to her stomach.

He moved a little bit closer. She could see the tiny freckles on his nose, feel his warm breath on her cheek and certainly smell his fresh aftershave. Her senses were scrambled. Was he about to kiss her?

'I think your PR campaign has just taken off in an unexpected way,' he whispered as he unfurled the newspaper.

She was muddled for a sec. The kiss wasn't coming. Her eyes tried to fixate on the coloured picture on the front of the red-top newspaper.

The effect was instantaneous. She sat bolt upright just as the text sounded on her phone.

The photo looked staged. It was just too perfect. Rose with her Doris Day–style dress and blonde hair streaming behind her and Will in his casual shirt and trousers. But it was the expressions on their faces that gave everything away—they were laughing and the elements of pure joy shone from their faces, in perfect unison with the pink and silver heart-shaped balloons escaping into the sky behind them.

If Rose worked in PR for the movies, she would have paid a fortune for a shot like this.

But it was the headline that took her breath away. *Has the Runaway Groom finally found his bride?*

'What?' She snatched the paper from his hands. 'What on earth is this?'

Will opened his mouth to speak but nothing sensible came out. 'I'm not sure… It's just a picture… It will blow over in a couple of days.'

The paper was crumpling beneath her fingers. Rose worked in PR. She knew exactly how big this was. She also hated the fact it was her face staring back at her from the front of the newspapers. It brought back horrible memories of a few years ago when she'd made every front page. She'd hated every second of that and never wanted to repeat it again. 'How many, Will? How many calls have you had this morning?'

He flinched. 'About a dozen.'

'A dozen!' She was shrieking and she couldn't help it. If it was any other girl—any other girl in the world right now photographed with Will— she'd be doing a happy dance. This would be a great kick-start for the publicity for the homeless charity.

But it wasn't any other girl. It was her. And she hated the fact this could blow out of proportion. Hated the fact it was her in the headlines. How ironic. She hated the media but had learned how to use them to her advantage. Maybe this was a wake-up call for her? Maybe she'd started to get a little complacent?

Something twisted inside her. 'Violet,' she breathed.

Will's cool hand touched her arm. 'I called her. She laughed. And warned me off again.'

'She laughed?' Rose could feel the waves of panic washing over her. She hadn't even hinted to

Violet the thoughts that were clamouring through her head about Will. How on earth could she? She couldn't make sense of them herself. The last thing she wanted to do was tell her sister she was falling for the Runaway Groom.

'All those calls I made this morning. Just wait until your exes see this. They'll think I'm next on your hit list. They'll think I'm just doing this because you've sucked me in.'

'Sucked me in how?' His voice was low and tinged with anger. He reached over and grabbed the newspaper from her hands. 'You know what they say about this—today's news, tomorrow's chip paper. It's a photo snapped by someone at the wedding exhibition yesterday. There's nothing we can do about it.' He shrugged his shoulders. 'If you go to a public place there's always a danger you'll get papped. You must be used to it.'

He had no idea. No idea what had happened a few years ago and how it had changed everything for her. Changed how she felt about herself. Changed how she thought her parents felt about her.

She took a deep breath and tried to think logically.

He was making sense but she couldn't even acknowledge it. 'But this is a disaster. What happens when I phone those women back? What if they refuse to participate because of this?' She pointed at the paper again. She hadn't even read the whole article. 'I mean, it's all rubbish.'

'No. It isn't.'

She turned quickly to his voice. Will was still lying on the bed. He reached up his hand and pulled her back down next to him.

'What are you talking about?' She couldn't help the tremble in her voice. They were back in their original position. Lying on the bed next to each other with only a few inches between their faces.

'Rose, stop pretending that nothing is happening between us. We both know that it is.' He lifted his finger and touched the side of her cheek, oh, so gently. She shivered. She couldn't believe he'd actually just said it. Acknowledged it out loud.

She wasn't going crazy. She wasn't imagining things. He felt it, too.

But he'd felt it four times before. History proved that. She didn't want to be number five.

This was the one and only time she'd felt like this.

Part of it was horrible. Last time she'd felt this vulnerable was after her friend's death when she'd been splashed all over the media.

Rose had learned quickly it was better to be the person to try and control the PR, than the person *in* the PR.

And the more her feelings grew for this guy, the more she questioned herself and her ability to trust her instincts. What had happened three years ago had affected her more than she'd ever realised. She would always regret leaving her friend. She would always regret the fact she hadn't hung around when there was even a possibility that Autumn could have put herself in harm's way. She'd spent the last three years playing the *if only* game.

And she couldn't afford to do that any more. She had to live in the real world.

And only her parents really knew that she'd been aware of Autumn's drug-taking. What would Will think of her if he knew the truth? If she revealed all her flaws to him?

'Why couldn't you just be an ordinary guy?' she whispered.

Will smiled. He was so much more laid-back about this. He didn't seem to have a single problem trusting his instincts—and that was probably part of the problem. What was more he didn't have a shadow of doubt in his eyes. Not like the clenched hand she currently felt protecting her heart.

'Why couldn't you just be an ordinary girl?'

He leaned forward and brushed his lips against hers. She was scared to move at first. Acknowledging it was one thing. Seeing where it might take them was entirely another.

But everything he did was completely natural. From edging closer so their bodies were touching, to his hands wandering through her hair and around her face and neck. Each kiss was designed to lead on to the next. To make her want more. And she did. *So* much more.

All the sensations in her body were on fire. As if Will had more than one set of hands and they were currently skimming her erogenous zones as if he were reaching out and kissing and caressing each one in turn.

Rose pulled back sharply.

'What's wrong?' Little creases appeared around his eyes.

'I don't know. I'm just nervous. I'm not sure about any of this.'

'What part are you not sure about?'

Her hand was resting on his bicep. She could feel the heat of his skin through her palm. Every sense in her wanted to run her hand up under the short sleeve of his shirt and feel more.

'I'm not a spotlight kind of girl, Will. I agreed to help you with the PR but I don't want PR for myself.'

She felt him suck in a deep breath. 'I'm afraid with me it might be part of the package. We could release a statement about your parents' renewal.

That would explain why we were there. They may well leave you alone after that.'

Forget about it. Forget about everything. Act on impulse, Rose, and just kiss him the way you really want to.

But she couldn't. For Rose this was all about control. Since her friend's death she'd become a control freak. It was why she did the job so well for the band. Nothing left to chance.

Now people were taking pictures of her she didn't know about. Pictures of her that told the whole world exactly how she felt about Will.

And the whole world exactly how he felt about her.

It was like a jolt—and probably just as well she was already lying down.

Her silence had obviously worried him. 'Am I overstepping the mark, Rose? Do you want me to leave you alone?'

'No.' It was the first concrete thought in her head.

She was so confused right now. She didn't want to be the next girl to be swept along in the flurry of love that surrounded Will Carter.

She wanted a chance to be normal. To be just Rose and just Will. Two people that were attracted to each other. The electricity sparking between them was everywhere. But while this was all new to her, every precautionary bone in her body kept reminding her it wasn't for Will.

And no matter which way she looked at it—it hurt.

'I can't be number five.' Her words came out solidly. Definitely.

Will looked sad as he shook his head. 'You're not number anything. You're Rose.' His hand touched her cheek again. 'Can't we see where this relationship takes us?'

'But that's just it, Will. You don't have relationships. You have engagements, wedding plans and then nothing. You're a commitment-phobe—even though you can't see it for yourself. I can't set myself up for that. I don't want to start a relationship that won't ever go anywhere.'

'That won't happen, Rose.' She'd expected him to say something different. She'd expected him to crack a joke about her being way too keen and these things being years away. He couldn't possibly know the surge of terrifying emotions in her chest.

She could see him trying to find the words and the thought he was trying to placate her made her wish the ground would open up and swallow her. Even saying those few words had been too much. She should have known better. She shouldn't even have acknowledged anything between them.

'This is different.' His words were unexpected. But she just couldn't let herself believe them— no matter how much she wanted to.

'I bet you've said that before.'

The wave of hurt on his face was obvious. And even though she should probably want to take the words back, she just didn't. It had to be said. Will's reputation had gone before him. It didn't matter that her own experience of him felt entirely different. For all she knew, all the other girls had thought that, too.

Will sat up on the bed as her phone beeped again. 'I don't know how to show you this is different, Rose. I don't know how to explain.'

She sat up and pulled out her phone. It was from her father.

Can you come and see me? There's something special I want you to do for me.

'It's my dad. I'd better go.'

Will nodded reluctantly. 'Rose?'

She'd already started towards the door. She hated the way she spun around, desperate to hang onto his words.

'Let's just see. Let's just see where this takes us.'

She couldn't speak. She couldn't even explain to herself why she felt so hurt. She just gave a reluctant nod before she disappeared out of the door and the hot tears started to snake down her cheeks.

Her dad was waiting for her in the kitchen, sketching with deep concentration on a bit of paper.

'Hi, Dad, what's up?'

His eyes narrowed for a second when he lifted his head. He'd always been able to read her like a book. She could see him think about asking her what was wrong, but the paper in front of him was a definite distraction.

He hesitated, then pushed it towards her. 'What do you think?'

It was a pencil drawing of a bangle with little scribbles next to each part. Three strands of gold in different colours pleated together with a little flower intersecting the pleat at each third of the bangle—a rose, a daisy and a violet.

'It's beautiful, Dad. What's this for?'

His well-worn face sagged in relief. 'It's for your mother. It's her gift for her wedding day. I wanted to give her something special. You will make it for me, won't you? And you'll be able to get the yellow, white and rose gold?'

Something surged inside her. Even though alarm bells were sounding all around her head about the amount of time the bangle would take to make, and the intricate details, there was just no way she could ever say no to her father.

The thing that struck her most was the absolute love she could recognise on his face. The fact that he'd spent a lot of time and effort on this design was obvious. But what was even more evident was just how much he loved her mum. After all these years he still wanted to do something to make her heart sing.

That was what she wanted. That was the kind of relationship she wanted. That was the kind of love she wanted. One that would last for ever.

She felt a tear spring to her eye again as her dad put his arm around her shoulder. 'Don't worry, Dad, I've got the three kinds of gold. It will be perfect. Mum will love it.'

But now that he'd sorted out his wedding gift her father's attentions had shifted immediately. Rick Cross was no fool. Particularly when it came to Rose.

'So what's wrong? What's going on with you and that Will Carter? Violet's moping around like a lost cause.'

'She is?'

'Of course she is. You've stolen her favourite pet.'

A tear slid down her cheek as everything just threatened to spill out. 'But I haven't. I was helping him—and he was helping me with the wedding arrangements. It's just that we've been spending so much time together. I didn't mean to leave Violet out. I'll phone her—no, I'll go and see her.' She was babbling and she just couldn't help it. Wasn't it Will that normally did this?

Her father shook his head. 'Rose? What's wrong? I was only joking. Violet can take care of herself. I just wondered if there was something I should know. My daughters seem to be getting married in short order these days.'

Rose felt her breath catch in her throat and her father noticed immediately. She'd just had that awkward conversation with Will. A conversation nobody should be having after such a ridiculously short amount of time. It was almost as if her father could read her mind—and heaven knew what he could find in there!

But Rick Cross was cooler than your average dad. 'I like that fella. Always knew nothing would happen between Violet and him. But you?' He gave a little shrug of his shoulders. 'I guess that depends how you feel.'

He left the words hanging in the air. It was awful. She wasn't ready to have that kind of conversation with her dad. He was still her *dad*. Then again, she wasn't ready to have that conversation with anyone.

She focused back on the drawing. 'Leave this with me. This will be fine.' Where she would find the hours from she had no idea. But if this was what her father wanted—this was what he would get.

If he noticed the abrupt subject change he didn't say anything. She picked up her bag. 'Oh, I forgot to tell you—the guy you wanted to write your biography, Tom Buckley from New York? He emailed today to agree the terms and conditions. He'll have full access to the band tour backstage. I'm just arranging flights for him now.'

A huge smile broke across her dad's face. This was something that was really important to him and he'd been quite insistent about who he wanted to do the job. Just as well Rose had worked with Tom in the past and could use her maximum persuasion skills—along with a hefty salary—to persuade him to write the biography in the timeframe her dad needed. One more ticked box and another thing off her plate. She felt a little surge of pride. Her dad was happy with her.

Her dad gave her a hug and a kiss. 'That's great, honey. Thanks for doing that. Now, if there's anything you need to talk about, come and see me. Or pick up the phone and I'm there.'

Her heart gave a little squeeze. He wouldn't pry. He wouldn't interrogate her. Just as well, as she didn't know what to say. But it was her dad's way of letting her know that he'd noticed.

He'd noticed something was wrong. Dads didn't come much better than Rick Cross. When the whole press thing had blown up when Autumn had overdosed he'd been her biggest ally—her best spokesperson. And he'd done exactly the same for Violet when her sex-tape scandal had hit the press. Rick Cross didn't take kindly to people trying to hurt his family.

He'd taken Rose in the car to see her friend's parents. He'd spent hours talking to them and comforting them—but in no way letting them blame Rose for their daughter's actions. And when the press had started to get nasty a few days later he'd made lightning-fast arrangements and got her out of there. She was lucky that her family were so supportive.

It gave her a little strength. A little fortitude. Maybe it was time to look at herself again. Maybe it was time to start trusting her instincts?

Her father had just told her he liked Will Carter. Will had been Violet's best friend for the last three years. And the man she knew in person didn't measure up to what she'd read in the press.

She reached over and gave her dad a quick hug. 'This bangle will be perfect. I'll make sure of it. Don't worry, Dad. You can trust me.'

He brushed a kiss against her cheek and gave her a curious look. 'Always, Rose.' Before he walked across the kitchen he paused in the doorway. 'Rose?' She looked up again and he gave her a rueful smile. 'When you know—you just know,' and then he turned and walked away, leaving her with the drawing clutched in her hands.

CHAPTER EIGHT

FOUR HUNDRED AND sixty emails. That was how many he had to read. Will groaned and put his head in his hands. This was getting out of control.

He couldn't concentrate. He couldn't focus. Because his head was so full of Rose.

The sensation he'd felt the other day at the wedding fair with Rose had swamped him. The words Rick Cross had said at their first meeting were echoing around his brain. *When you know, you just know.* But it was more than that. It was the way Rick had looked at Sherry, too. The zing between them. He'd never had that before. But he had it with Rose.

Trouble was, he didn't know what to do next. How on earth could he convince Rose that everything about this just felt different—just felt right?

He didn't blame her. He really didn't. How would he feel if Rose had been engaged before?

He was lucky she would even stay in the same room as him.

But he just couldn't help how he felt about her. It was taking over every waking minute of his life. He looked at the calendar, then walked over to the window. The island was right in front of him and from this view he could see the roof of the church. Something curled inside him.

A tiny seed of an idea. A wild idea. A crazy idea.

If he told Violet she'd probably dunk him in a bath of ice. If he told Rose she would run screaming for the hills...

For the first time ever Will felt as if he could see himself grow old with someone. It should be terrifying. But instead a warm feeling spread across his chest.

And something about this idea was taking shape in his head. He only had to do one thing. One thing that he hoped no one would find out about.

And it could make all the difference to his life.

Rose put the phone down and laid her head on the desk.

'Was it that bad?' Violet was standing laughing at the door with her arms folded.

Rose didn't even lift her head. 'Worse,' she sighed.

Violet walked over and lifted up the piece of paper on Rose's desk. First it was a gasp of shock, then it was a snort, then it was just a peal of laughter. By the time Rose lifted her head Violet was wiping a tear from her eye.

'I came up to tell you Will's just pulled into the car park. I bet you can't wait to tell him what all his dares are.' She shook her head as she kept looking at the list. 'I can't wait to see his face.'

'Really?' She half hoped Violet wasn't joking. 'Then you can tell him.'

She raised her eyebrows. 'Oh, no, girl. That's your job.' She gave Rose a nod of her head and walked back to the door with her shoulders shaking.

Rose heard the murmur of words down the corridor as she obviously met Will. A few minutes later he appeared at the door, face pale. 'Oh, no. What have they suggested?'

Rose gestured towards the seat opposite her. 'You better sit down.'

For once Will did exactly as he was told.

She started carefully. 'The good thing is that these will definitely generate media interest.'

'And the bad news?'

She gulped as she passed over the piece of paper. 'You might not like some of them.' She bit her lip. 'The thing is, the newspaper already knows about all the dares. So we can't get any-one to change them.'

His brow wrinkled. 'Why would they need to be changed? Are any of them going to kill me?'

She shook her head swiftly. 'No. No. That was one of the conditions they were given—nothing fatal.'

'Please tell me that you're joking.'

She shook her head again and gave him a half-smile. 'Eh, no.'

'Dangling from Tower Bridge and getting dunked in the Thames?'

Rose tried not to smile. There was no doubt the press would have a field day with these. To say nothing of all the TV and media interviews she'd arranged for the ex-fiancées. This could end up being one of the most successful PR campaigns she'd ever been involved in.

Will had been right. Three out of four of his exes had been fine. And even Melissa had started to come round. She was gearing herself up for TV interviews and appeared to be quite happy at the prospect.

'Dress for a day as a gladiator/warrior and pa-rade around Piccadilly Circus? Wear a thong and work in a women's underwear department for the day?' His voice was getting more incredulous as he continued to read.

Rose couldn't help but start laughing. 'Those

last two came from Angie and Marta. They were definitely going more for the laughs than the cold, hard revenge.'

Two of Will's ex-fiancées were now married with children. They were happy to help the charity auction and had obviously had fun thinking up what he should do. Both of them had seemed very nice and very happy with their lives.

The third, Esther, had looked on it as good publicity for her new TV-presenting career. She'd been quite mercenary about it. She wasn't that interested in the charity but she was certainly interested in raising her profile.

Will slumped further down the chair as he finished reading. 'A full body wax on live TV?' The paper was now crumpled in his hand. 'Which do you think will win?' he said resignedly.

Rose tried to be rational. 'I think it's a toss-up between a dunking in the Thames and the man thong.' She held a scrap of luminous green material with her pen. 'Look. Marta tried to be really helpful. She even sent the thong.'

Will's eyes nearly popped out of his head as he reached forward and snatched the tiny item. 'You have got to be joking. There's absolutely no way on this earth I'm ever putting that on. Or dressing like a blooming gladiator.'

But Rose was on her feet in an instant. 'Oh, no, you don't. You agreed to this. This isn't about you. This is about the charity. Think how much money will be raised by people phoning in to vote on this stuff. I bet you'll be able to employ some new workers. Don't start being a wuss on me now.'

He groaned and sagged down again, staring at the thong in his hand. 'But people won't be talking about the charity. People will be talking about me and my utter humiliation.'

'So what?' She was feeling annoyed now. This had taken time, effort and persuasive skills she hadn't even known she had. 'It will also raise the profile of your charity—which, if you remember, was exactly the brief you gave me.'

His eyes fixed on hers. For a second it seemed he was assessing her. If he found her wanting she would find the nearest vase and whack him over the head again.

He stood up. His imposing figure in front of hers. His broad chest filling her vision. His voice had a determined edge to it. 'It has to be about more than this. It has to be something else.'

'What? What else do you want from me, Will?' she shouted, all patience finally lost. 'What else can I do?'

'I want a night.'

'What?' She was losing the plot. None of this made sense to her any more. She had too much going on. Too much to think about. Sisters, fathers, mothers, weddings, band tours, bangles, promotion, interviews, Will, Will and more Will.

Any minute now she would spontaneously combust.

But Will was on a roll. 'I want a night. I want to show people what this is really about. I want to spend a night on the streets the way my friend had to when he was homeless—when he didn't know where to turn. I want people to understand how terrifying and dangerous it can be. I want to give them a real feel for the vulnerability—and the stories—of the people I want to help.'

Her brain started spinning. It was genius. It was perfect. It would complement the other publicity perfectly. People might have fun voting, but if they watched something like that it would really bring the message home. But when he'd said the words 'I want a night' it wasn't quite what she'd hoped to hear. And now she was annoyed with herself for even imagining he might have meant something else.

Will was still mumbling. 'And I want you to do it with me.'

The words clicked into place in her brain. 'Me?'

'Yes. You.'

She was baffled. 'But why?' Could her head really get any more confused?

'Because you're the perfect person to do it

with. People know who you are. A famous couple's daughter? They'll love it. They'll think it's something that a girl like you, and—' he pointed to himself '—a guy like me would never do. Let's show them how hard it is. Let's show them just how difficult it is. Let's tell them some of the stories of the people out there.'

Boy, when he wanted it, his charm just came out in spades. And it was rational, businesslike sense. It put another edge to the publicity. She kind of wished she'd thought of it herself. But she kind of wished he wanted to do it with someone else. Could she really put herself in the spotlight again?

His hands rested gently on her shoulders. She could smell him. His scent was invading her senses. It was like a magic potion winding its way around her. She could almost see its tendrils wrapping around her body and throwing all rational thoughts out of the window.

'I need you, Rose. I need to do this. And I need to do it with you. Do you understand that?'

There it was again. That way he made her stomach twist and turn. He knew just how to speak to her. Just how to reach in and touch the little parts of her that couldn't say no to him. Part of this terrified her.

She wasn't in a situation where she couldn't say no. She just didn't want to. And even though this was completely different from years ago, a tiny little bit of her still remembered feeling so distracted by a man she'd forgotten about everything else. The guilt still consumed her. She didn't ever want to be that way again.

It didn't matter this was Will. It didn't matter there was no element of danger. This wasn't about him. This was about *her*. And her ability to trust. She still hadn't completely learned to trust her instincts. And a guy with Will's history? He didn't really have trust stamped all over him.

Still, she couldn't ignore what was happening between them. She couldn't ignore the way her body reacted every time he was near. She'd never felt this way about a guy before. Was this what love felt like? Or was this just infatuation?

'Rose, are you okay? Do you need some time to think this over? Please tell me you'll think about it. I really want to do this with you.'

She took a deep breath. Was she prepared to do this for a charity? No matter how uncomfortable and scary it was? Of course she was. She was lucky. She'd had a privileged life. Her parents had always drummed into her and her sisters how lucky they were. They made a point of supporting their favourite charities and the work her mother did was never-ending. Of course she could spend one night on the streets.

She took a deep breath. This seemed like

so much more. It seemed like a partnership. It seemed like a way of cementing things between them—to see if their paths could truly connect or not.

'I'll do it.' There. She said the words before she had too much time to think any more. To mull things over.

And Will did the thing she'd longed for. He sealed it with a kiss.

The interviews were set. The voting lines would be announced tomorrow. With so much publicity for the homeless charity and the papers filled with all his ex-fiancées everyone seemed to have forgotten about the picture of him and Rose in the press. Everyone but him.

For the first time in his life he'd cut a picture from the press. He'd even saved it and printed it from one of the press Internet sites.

He loved it. He loved the way they were captured in it. Daisy was the photographer in Rose's family and he'd heard her talk with passion about her pictures and what she wanted to capture in them. But he'd never really got *it* before.

Not before now.

Not before he could see the look on both his and Rose's faces. Captured for an eternity. And he loved it. He was actually going to frame it.

But it made him nervous. Now, everything else

paled in comparison to how he felt about Rose. He could see it now. He could see the infatuation. But he'd never felt the love. Not like this.

How would she be when he told her what he'd done? If she felt the same way he did, everything should work out fine. If she didn't?

He'd need to learn to live with having a runaway bride.

CHAPTER NINE

PAUL SCHOLAND WAS her favourite ever TV presenter. With his bright, sparkling blue eyes and prematurely grey hair the female audience just loved him. He had all the exes eating out of the palm of his hand and had got the mixture of personal and publicity just right. Rose's tightly tied-up stomach was finally starting to relax. Particularly when she got a text about the sudden upsurge in voting. Things were going better than she could ever have imagined.

Will had spent most of the morning pacing around the room; Violet had come in every now and then to howl with laughter at some of the comments and then left again. Will's segment had been pre-recorded and when his face filled the screen Rose took in a deep breath.

The camera loved him. She'd always known it, but she'd never really appreciated it before. His eyes were even more remarkable than Paul's, his dark hair framing his face, with tiny lived-in lines around his eyes enhancing his good looks. But better than everything was his easy, laid-back attitude. The whole world was falling in love with him right now—her included—and Rose was feeling sparks of jealousy.

This was her Will. Hers. She didn't want to share him.

'Is it over yet?' He was watching from beneath his fingers. She nodded. 'Just about.' She turned her phone towards him. 'Look how things have gone.'

His eyes widened and he dropped his hands. 'How much?'

She smiled. 'Yeah, that much. And it's only the first day. You were on the front page of one of the red tops today, too. People are talking about this—talking about your charity.'

He looked a little doubtful. 'I'm being made a laughing stock on national TV.'

Rose stood up and walked towards him. 'Paul handled those interviews really well. In the meantime, money is being raised for your charity. You've got another interview on the main news channel tomorrow. That will give you an opportunity to speak about your friend and why you're doing this. You'll be able to talk about the night on the street, too. It will all balance out, Will. This is a good thing that you're doing.'

He stood up next to her. 'I know. I just wonder

what I'm going to end up doing.' He shook his head. 'It could be a disaster.'

'It will be fine. No matter what it is at the end of the day, it'll be worth it.'

He nodded slowly. 'You're right. Of course you're right.' He lifted his hand and twisted his finger through a lock of her hair. 'So where are we with your list?'

For a second her thoughts were jumbled, then her woolly brain came into focus. 'The wedding list, yes.' She turned and walked over to the table and picked up her black planner. 'Okay, venue, marquees, food, band all sorted.'

'Is your dad playing at his own wedding?'

She sighed. 'Of course he is. But not till later. Their support band is playing for most of the main event. But there's no show without punch. At some point my dad and the guys will want to get up there and rock out.'

She ran her finger down the rest of the list. 'Violet's doing the flowers—apparently my mother's already given her instructions. Mum's got her dress and we've all picked ours. Daisy is doing some of the wedding pics and her assistant is doing some others.'

'What about everything else?'

'Well, the wedding favours and chocolates are sorted, as are the chair covers and balloons. I've just got to sort out a wedding cake and to choose wine and a drinks list for the bar.'

'When do you need to do that?'

She wrinkled her nose. 'In around an hour. I was kind of hoping you would come with me and help me choose the last few things.'

Will shrugged. 'I can choose wedding cake and the wine is already sorted. Sounds like every guy's dream date.'

She opened her mouth to stop him, to tell him it wasn't a date, and then stopped. She was almost glad he was thinking like that. It felt kind of nice.

She took a few minutes to finish up with emails and phone calls, finalising the flight arrangements for the reporter flying in from New York to write her father's book. She'd worked with Tom Buckley on numerous occasions and he was great. The only hiccup this time was the scheduling. Tom was on another job and the soonest he could get here was the same day as her mother and father's wedding renewal. She'd have to leave at night to pick him up from the airport. It couldn't be helped.

Will finished on his phone around the same time she did. 'Ready?'

She nodded and they walked outside to his car. 'Do you have an address?'

She bit the inside of her cheek and turned her

phone around to show him. He blinked. Twice. 'Really? What on earth...?'

'Yeah, I know. When I phoned Angie to ask her to take part in setting a dare she asked me how things were. Before I knew it, I'd told her about my parents' wedding renewal and how difficult it was to find everyone at short notice. She said her sister would be delighted to make the wedding cake.'

'Does she know I'm coming along?'

Rose looked at him nervously. 'It might be a little awkward but I'm sure it will be fine.'

'I sure hope so. Otherwise we're both in trouble. You won't get any cake and I'll probably end up wearing some.'

She laughed. 'I'm sure it won't end up like that. Angie was great on the phone. She couldn't have been nicer. She seems really happy now she's married with a baby of her own.'

He looked thoughtful as they continued along the road. 'Angie is nice. She's great, in fact.'

The words did strange things to her insides. She liked Angie. She really did. She just didn't want to think about the history between her and Will. She couldn't even bear to think about it.

'She just wasn't right for me—like I wasn't right for her.'

It was like a wave of relief washing over her. And it was almost as if Will realised her apprehension because one of his hands left the wheel and squeezed her leg through her dress as he glanced sideways at her.

'You're right. I'm sure it will be fine.' He put his hand back on the steering wheel and they continued along the road until they eventually reached the address.

Angie's sister Deb was the ultimate professional. Small and petite with a bright red bob, she had a whole portfolio of cake photos to show Rose along with lots of samples of her baking.

They were all laid out before her. 'Here are the sponges—try a bit of each. If there's a special request I can make it. I have traditional fruit cake, carrot cake, chocolate cake, strawberry and white chocolate, dark chocolate and orange, coconut and vanilla sponge, lemon sponge and coffee sponge.' Each one was more delicious than the last.

'Do you like them?'

'I love them all.' Rose kept flicking through the cake book. It was difficult to know which style and what kind of decorations to choose. She turned the book towards Will. 'What do you think? A traditional tiered cake or something more novelty?'

'What do your parents like best?'

'That's just it. I don't know. For birthdays we

quite often have novelty cakes. But I'm not sure if they'd want that for their wedding.'

'How many tiers do you want? Do you know how many guests are coming?' Angie's sister had her order book poised.

Rose groaned. 'It could be three hundred.'

Deb blinked twice. 'Do you want some advice?'

Rose nodded. 'Gladly. I know nothing about this kind of stuff. I just don't have a clue.'

Deb flicked through her portfolio. 'Keep it simple—or as simple as you can with that amount of guests. How about an eight-tier cake with one of every kind of sponge? That way your guests will be able to find something they like. I can cover it in royal icing with some pale ribbons and you could get your florist to do a display for the top that matches your mum's flowers.'

Rose nodded quickly. She was happy to take any suggestion right now that made things a little easier. Deb pointed to the cakes in front of her. 'I'll go and make you some tea. Just pick which sponge for each layer.' She handed over a diagram. 'Remember sponge one will be the biggest and sponge eight the smallest so all you need to do is decide the order. I'll give you some space because this can take a little bit of time.'

She left Rose and Will together in the room.

Will had barely said a word since they got there. 'Are you okay?'

He gave the tiniest nod. 'It's just weird, that's all. She hasn't even mentioned the dares or the press stuff.'

'She probably doesn't want to.' Rose pointed to all the sponges. 'This is her business and doing Mum and Dad's cake will be good publicity for her portfolio. I'm expecting her to charge a lot more because of the short notice but I'm just so relieved to have someone.'

Will frowned. 'This wedding is costing a lot of money.'

Rose nodded.

'But doesn't that kind of go against your mum and dad's principles?'

She wrinkled her nose. 'I know what you mean. To be honest they probably give away the same amount of money that they spend.' She shrugged. 'From a strictly PR perspective the wedding will look ostentatious. It will feed the public image that they're successful and doing well. But it also means that they can continue to give to all the charitable causes they want to— with or without publicity.'

Will nodded. He looked thoughtful and picked up a piece of one of the sponges. 'Which is your favourite?'

'I can't decide. They're all delicious.'

'What would you pick for your wedding cake?' It was a simple enough question. 'If it was up to me I'd have the whole thing chocolate.'

'Oh, no.' She waved her hand. 'I wouldn't want a wedding cake anyway.'

'You wouldn't?' He was surprised. He knew she'd said she didn't want a big wedding. But just how small did she actually mean?

Rose shook her head and waved her hand. 'I don't want any of it. Any of it at all.'

A horrible feeling crept over him. 'Do you mean the wedding?'

She tilted her head to the side. 'No, but that's all I want. The wedding. A dress and a bunch of flowers for my hands.'

He raised his eyebrows. 'And presumably a groom?'

She threw back her head and laughed. 'Well, hopefully that's part of the package and not an optional extra.'

Relief started to flood through him. It was odd. He hadn't actually realised that when Rose said small, she actually meant minimal. It wasn't quite what he'd imagined. But the more he got to know her, the more he understood.

Rose lifted a little piece of carrot cake and nibbled. 'This one is delicious.' She sighed and lifted up the strawberry and white chocolate. 'But I like this one, too.' It crumbled as she bit into it and Will reached over and put his hand under her chin. She spluttered as he caught the crumbs. 'Never thought of you as a messy eater.' His eyes twinkled as he lifted some of the chocolate cake. 'Here, try my favourite.'

She hesitated. There was something so intimate about being fed by someone else. Even if it was in the middle of the day in someone else's house. Her eyes darted to the door. Deb was nowhere in sight.

She opened her mouth as he positioned the light, moist sponge at her mouth. The chocolate frosting was perfect, sending little explosions around her mouth, to say nothing of the ones as his fingers contacted her lips.

His thumb smudged across the edges. 'You've got a little bit stuck,' he whispered.

'Where?' She looked around for a napkin.

'I'll get it,' he offered as he bent forward to kiss her. His lips touched hers, lightly at first, delicately, before he eased her lips apart and joined their mouths together. His hand slid around the nape of her neck and through her hair, making her want to beg for more. This was it. This was what he did to her. Gave her a little taste that left her begging for more.

The voices started in her head. She was getting in too deep. Every kiss took her a step closer to never wanting to go back. *Angie's sister's house* floated around her head. There was a thought to chill her heated blood. She pulled back and made a grab for a napkin. It was perfect timing as Deb appeared with the tea, her bright smile still firmly in place.

Rose picked up the diagram and quickly numbered each tier of the cake with the sponge she wanted. 'Thank you so much, Deb, for doing this. Let me know how much I owe you.'

Deb hesitated but shook her head. 'It's fine, but I'd be really grateful if you could get a photo with your mum and dad and the cake for my portfolio.'

'Of course. Of course. No problem at all.'

Deb gave a hopeful smile. 'Thanks.'

It only took them a few minutes to get in the car and leave. Rose was feeling happy. All the things on her wedding list were finally ticked off. For once, she could relax. All she needed to focus on now was making the bangle for her mum.

Then there was the horrible sinking realisation that she really had no reason to spend time with Will any more. All of a sudden his proposition about being on the streets one night didn't seem quite so scary.

Will seemed laid-back. 'So, are you ready for your night on the tiles with me?'

'When a guy invites a girl for a night on the tiles he doesn't usually mean it literally.'

Will glanced over at her. 'I like to do things a

little differently. Anyway it will take my mind off those hideous dares. Have you heard any more about them?'

She nodded and smiled. 'It's a definite split vote between the gladiator, the thong and the total body waxing.' She shrugged. 'Personally I thought people might be more inclined to go for the more venomous one—the dunking in the Thames. But no, it seems it's humiliation all the way.'

'Does the total-body hair wax include the hair on my head?'

'Absolutely.'

He shuddered. 'It just doesn't seem that appropriate for a homeless charity.'

'But dressing in a thong and working in a lingerie department does?'

His eyes were fixed on the road but his lips turned upwards. 'No, that's definitely pure humiliation all the way.'

He was taking it really well. The whole dare thing didn't seem to bother him or annoy him. He was prepared to take it on the chin.

It was just another reason to like him all the more. Somehow she knew spending a night out on the streets with Will wasn't going to be the best idea in the world. He was already ticking so many boxes for her. Was she really prepared to let him tick the last few?

'What will I need?'

'Warm clothes, especially a jacket and shoes. It can be really cold at night.'

'Do you think we'll get any sleep at all?'

'I have no idea. I guess we'll find out. Is one of the reporters from the paper coming along?'

She screwed up her face. 'He'll do a cover story. It took quite a bit of persuading. But I don't think he'll stay all night.'

Will's phone sounded and he lifted his hip slightly. 'Can you pull that out for me?'

She stretched over and slid her hand into his pocket. The skin next to the thin cotton lining of the pocket was warm. She tried not to focus on that as she made a grab for the phone. She pulled it out and glanced at the screen.

'It's Violet. She wants you to phone her.' Her stomach did a little flip. This was her sister. Will was Vi's best friend. She had no reason to feel jealous.

Will gave a slight nod of his head but said nothing. It just made her feel worse.

'Just drop me back at home,' she said abruptly. 'I need to spend some time on my mother's bangle.'

'Okay.' They drove in silence until he reached her parents' house and she jumped out of the car as quickly as she could. 'Thanks. I'll text you about Saturday night.' She slammed the door quickly as she strode inside, passing Violet in the corridor. 'Is Will outside? I need to talk to him.'

Violet wandered past her and outside as Rose made her way to her workshop. She needed to get a hold of herself. She needed to get things into perspective. Her mind was playing tricks on her these days. Making her think irrational thoughts. Was this what it felt like to be in love? Because if it was—it wasn't good. All of a sudden she felt sick to her stomach.

There was no getting away from it. Saturday night on the streets was going to be make or break for her and Will. He knew it. And she knew it.

CHAPTER TEN

IT WAS THE final dress fitting. Daisy was back now with her ever expanding tiny bump. The green dress covered it to perfection and standing side by side the three sisters in their green, blue and purple dresses made a striking picture.

Sherry clapped her hands. 'Oh, my beautiful girls. You all look perfect.'

Rose tugged at her hair. 'Do we need a tiara or a fascinator or something?'

Sherry exchanged a look with Violet. 'We've got that all under control. You'll have a fresh flower for your hair.'

Daisy was distracted. She sat down and eyed her jewelled sandals suspiciously. 'Can I wear Converse instead?'

'No,' Sherry said swiftly. She held up an alternative pair of flat jewelled sandals. 'I've got you flatties for the night. You only need to wear the heels for the renewal vows.'

Sherry turned to Rose. 'Everything is ready? Everything is done?'

Rose nodded and started to reel everything off. 'Marquees will be set up the day before. Violet's taking care of the flowers, Daisy the photographs. Dad's backup band is organised. The chairs and tables come the day before. The favours and cake are organised—along with the menu. Everything will be perfect, Mum, you don't need to worry about a thing.'

Sherry enveloped her in a hug. 'That's why we trust you with everything, honey. You're just so good at organising. I don't know what we'd do without you.'

Rose beamed; she didn't even know about the bangle yet. Her mother would be delighted. But Violet didn't look delighted. Violet looked mad. As if her mother's words had just irked her.

Rose had no idea what was going on. But she'd too much to think about right now.

And most of her thoughts were around a runaway groom…

He could hardly even see her face. The hood of her parka came right down over her nose. He stuck his face inside. 'Is anyone alive in here?'

'You said it would be cold. I'm just trying to make sure I'll be warm.'

He slid his arm around her shoulders. 'It will be cold. But I'll do my best to keep you warm.'

She glanced around. There were a number of

people in the homeless shelter drinking tea and soup. 'What time does this place close?'

'Eleven.'

'And where does everyone go then?' She was looking around at the array of figures in the room. Most weren't dressed very well; all of them were in layers. He saw her look down and knew exactly what she'd see. Lots of the people who slept on the streets had shoes that were mismatched and falling apart. Once they found a pair of shoes that fitted they wore them until they literally fell off their feet.

'That's just the point. I guess we'll find out.'

Rose inched a little closer to him. Will was used to coming here. He often came and helped out in the food kitchen. He wasn't fazed by the sometimes unkempt people that used it. This place was a safe haven. Somewhere they could be fed and get a few hours' warmth. It was staffed completely by volunteers and Will would like nothing more than for it to be open for longer.

As the staff in the kitchen started to clean and tidy up Will moved forward to help. Rose was right by his side, washing dishes and cleaning worktops. It was all hands on deck here.

By the time they locked the front doors darkness had fallen. Rose was glancing around at the people gathered in small clumps around the door.

Few words were exchanged. Most were trying to decide where to stay safe for the night.

'I had no idea so many people stayed on the streets,' she whispered. 'Can't they get emergency accommodation from the council?'

Will shook his head. 'Some of these people have been through the system—some haven't. A few have addiction problems and weren't able to manage a tenancy even though the council had found one for them. Managing money is a skill that some people find really difficult. There's just not enough support out there.'

A thin, wiry teenage boy walked past, head down and hands in his pockets. Rose sucked in a breath. 'Will,' she whispered, 'he doesn't even look sixteen.'

Will's heart squeezed. 'That's Alfie. And he's seventeen. He's been on the streets for the last two years and he won't let me help him. I've tried.'

Rose looked horrified. 'Why on earth would a kid that age end up on the streets?'

Will shook his head. 'That's just it. He won't say. And he's one of about twenty kids I know that really shouldn't be here.' He nudged her with his elbow and pointed across the road. 'That's Danny, one of the voluntary workers. He'll spend most of the night keeping watch over the young ones to try and keep them safe. He's a real god-send.'

Rose's brow was wrinkled and she turned to face him. 'I don't get it. Why don't these kids want to be under a roof and sleeping in a bed?'

'Because not all homes are like yours and mine. Not all homes are safe. I suspect some of these kids have come through the care system and slipped through the net. Others are escaping abuse. Some have mental health disorders that make it difficult for them to cope.' He looked around and pointed towards a group of middle-aged men. 'And it's not just the young ones. Last year they estimated around three thousand people slept rough in London, people who just don't have family or friends to help them. Lots of them ended up homeless because of redundancy or domestic abuse. There's a whole host of different reasons people end up like this.'

Rose slipped her hand into his. 'Your friend. How is he?'

Will felt himself bristle. It was the whole reason he was here but it was still a sore point. He still felt as if he'd let his friend down. 'He's getting there. It took a long time before he'd let anyone help him. That's just it. I could stand here in the street and announce I'd give everyone somewhere safe to sleep for the night but most of them wouldn't believe me—wouldn't trust me. They wouldn't come.' His voice was tinged with sadness as Rose's fingers curled around his own. He couldn't imagine being here with anyone else. He couldn't ever have imagined any of his previous girlfriends agreeing to do this with him—he wouldn't have wanted them to.

But this was different. This was important to him. And if the decision he'd made about Rose was right, this was the kind of thing he needed to share with her—he needed her to understand.

He pointed to the dark streets. 'Are you sure you're okay with this?' She looked nervous, even though she was obviously trying her best not to.

'I'm fine,' she said quietly before adding, 'I'm with you.'

He nodded and took a few steps down the street. 'Then let's go. Let's see how you survive on the streets at night.'

This London was completely different from the London that Rose knew. She wasn't naïve. She knew people slept rough and there were homeless hostels all over London but, while she'd taken part in a lot of charity work with her parents, she'd never worked in any of these places.

London at night for Rose and her sisters had involved trendy streets and clubs. Coming out late at night, clamouring into a cab and grabbing some food from an eatery on the way home. The streets they were walking down now were unfamiliar to Rose. Dark, damp, creepy.

Will took her down alleyways, stopping by rubbish bins to speak to people hidden in the shadows. Handing out biscuits and cards with addresses for assistance. As the cold crept around them and the night became even darker they kept going. Tramping unfamiliar streets without fear. Occasionally they met other workers, voluntary organisations and a few cops on the beat. Will seemed to recognise most of them, stopping to compare notes and talk about trouble spots. A few made jokes about his press coverage, though all thanked him for trying to raise the issue.

Fatigue started to settle in. Her muscles were tiring. The cold was creeping down to her very bones. Will steered her towards one of the bridges spanning the Thames. 'This is a hotspot,' he murmured. 'Lots of people sleep under this bridge at night. Stay close. Fights sometimes break out.'

The rain had started to fall. Thick, heavy drops that soaked straight through her jacket. They hurried under the bridge. There was no lighting under here. It was almost completely black with only a flicker from the occasional match somewhere.

At the other side there was a fight starting over some cardboard boxes. Rose drew close to Will, wrapping her arms around his waist and shielding her face away. The fight ended as quickly as it had started, with the victor claiming his spoils and arranging his cardboard box on the ground.

'They were fighting over a cardboard box?' Rose whispered.

Will nodded. 'You've no idea what has value on the street. Especially on a night like this. Here.' He pulled her over to the wall under the bridge and pulled her down next to him. The cold concrete quickly wound its way through her clothes and she shifted on the ground. Will still had his arm around her shoulders and she snuggled closer to get some body heat. 'Are we going to stay here?'

It all seemed so alien to her. So cold. So uncomfortable. So unsafe.

He nodded. 'This is it. This is where a lot of the people on the streets spend the night. How long do you think you could actually sleep for?'

'I don't think I can sleep at all,' she whispered, not wanting to offend any of the huddled figures around her.

'I know. But we have to try. We have to understand what it is these people go through every night. That's the message I want to get out there.'

Something struck her. 'What happened to the reporter?'

Will sighed. 'He got waylaid with something else. He interviewed me earlier and I've got a little camera attached to the pocket of my jacket. He should pick up some things from that.'

Rose put her hand on the freezing ground. 'But he won't pick up this. He won't pick up how cold it is out here. He won't get how the wind whistles under the bridge and the raindrops still reach you even though you're in the middle.'

Will smiled. 'But you do.'

Something fleeted across her face. 'Yeah, but I don't like it, Will. I'd be terrified if I was here myself. I can't stand the thought of living every night like this.'

He looked out over the darkness of the still water of the Thames. 'This is where Arral used to sleep at night.'

'Your friend?'

He nodded. 'I still can't fathom how it happened. How a guy who did so well at university, got his first job and flat just ended up on a downward spiral that ended up with him stabbed and in hospital.' He shook his head as he looked at the bodies huddled around them. 'Arral was married. But when he lost his job and his home, his wife just upped and left. She didn't take her vows seriously. The whole for better or worse part just seemed to pass her by. I've thought about it for the last few years. How marriage was about good and bad.' He squeezed his eyes shut for a second. 'It always made me second-guess things.

It always made me scrutinise my relationships. Would this person still want to grow old with me if I didn't have the fancy house, jobs and cars? It made me question my abilities to choose wisely.'

She frowned. 'But I've met all four of them. Marta and Angie seemed nice. Both of them weren't bitter. They knew they weren't destined to be with you. Esther is focused on her media career. And Melissa?' She shrugged. 'She seems to have her own demons. I doubt very much you can do anything about them.'

She squeezed his hand. 'This place gives you a whole new perspective on life, doesn't it?' She was looking around. Looking at the array of faces, some hidden beneath hoods or cardboard boxes. There was a real mixture of people here. Mainly young and middle-aged. There were around forty people under this bridge, but only two she would have termed elderly.

'Are you okay?'

She shivered and huddled a little closer. 'Yes. I'm just remembering, I guess.'

'Remembering what?'

'My friend, Autumn,' she said sadly. 'She died from a drug overdose at a party one night. We were both there, but I made bad choices that night. We both did.' Her voice started to shake. 'No one knows, Will. But I knew that Autumn had dabbled with drugs before. I knew and I still left her alone that night to go off with some guy. I wasn't a silly teenager. I was a twenty-four-year-old woman and I left my friend behind. I let her down. I let myself down. And I let my parents down. They had to deal with the fallout of my actions. They had to deal with my bad choices.' She was ashamed to say those words out loud. What would Will think of her now he knew all about her flaws? 'I wonder how many of these people didn't even get to make a choice to end up here?' she murmured. 'It seems so unfair.'

Will nodded. She couldn't really tell him how horrible she found this.

'I had family. I had a really strong family. My dad took over. He came with me to speak to Autumn's parents. He was there for hours.' She glanced up at Will. 'People just don't realise what my dad is made of. "Rock star" doesn't equate with supportive parent.' Will gave her shoulder a squeeze. 'But after the funeral was over I just couldn't take it. I couldn't take the bad press. I'm not a good person, Will. I'm the most flawed person you could meet.' She was shaking her head in disbelief.

'I went to New York to escape. To start again.' She held up her hand as the tears formed in her eyes. 'But now I feel a thoroughly pathetic human being. I didn't feel strong enough to cope—so I left. But what if you don't have the means to leave?' Her voice was starting to waver. 'Or what if the means to leave makes you end up on the street?' Being out here was scary. Having this as your reality must be terrifying for some of these people. 'I wasn't strong enough. I couldn't take what the press said about me. I hated having my picture in the paper. I couldn't take the lies. I didn't trust my judgement any more and I hated the fact that I felt as if I'd let my parents down. But I still had my family. I still had them around me. Is this what happens when you don't have family to support you?'

He tilted her chin up to face him. 'Rose, you and Violet are two of the strongest people I've ever met. The press has had a field day with you both. You, with your friend's death and Violet, with her leaked sex tape. But it hasn't dragged either of you down. If anything, it's made you both stronger. You didn't run away. You regrouped. You've spent the last few years working hard for your dad. You haven't hid away. And you've found something else. You've found something that you love—your jewellery making. And you've worked hard at that, too. How does that make you weak? How does that make you a failure? We've all got to take what life throws at us and deal with it the best we can.'

He stroked a finger down her face. 'Is this it, Rose? Is this what you're so afraid of? The press putting things you can't control about you in the papers? Letting your parents down? Trusting your judgement?'

He gave a gentle laugh. 'Have faith, Rose. Have faith in yourself. Because I have faith in you, and so does every member of your family. You've organised your parents' renewal vows in record time. *They* trusted *you* to do that.' He emphasised the words by pressing his palm against her chest. 'They trusted your judgement—even if you don't.' He leaned closer. 'And I trust your judgement, Rose, more than you can ever know.'

His face nuzzled against hers, his cold nose sending little delicious waves down her chilled bones. 'Do you think I would have brought anyone else here? Do you think any of my previous girlfriends would even have made an attempt to understand this?' She could hear the conviction in his voice. He really believed in what he was saying. 'It could only ever have been you, Rose. Just you. You're the only person I could share this with.'

He straightened a little. 'I told you about Arral and his wife leaving. I told you that in the lead-up to my weddings I started to have doubts. Doubts about whether I could see myself growing old with that person.' He touched her cheek. 'I don't have any doubts about you, Rose. I can see myself growing old with you. You've got to give us a chance. You've got to know that this is real between us.'

There they were. The words she'd thought she wanted to hear. Every ounce of him believed what he was saying. How could she tell him that even though he was sure, she was the one with doubts?

Realisation was seeping through her with the cold concrete beneath her. This wasn't really about him. This was about her.

Will might well be the Runaway Groom. It was a label that was never going to disappear. Every instinct told her to trust him. Every instinct told her to believe what he was saying.

But she hadn't learned to trust her instincts again yet. It was the one thing that was holding her back. The wary part of her brain said he was in the first flush of romance again. That in a few months none of this would be real. How well could you possibly know someone after a few weeks?

But then there was Daisy. She'd had one night with Seb and returned weeks later to give him baby news. They'd married in the space of a few weeks, and, while there might have been a few initial doubts, on their wedding day their faces hadn't lied. It was two people, totally in love with each other, who'd said those vows. If it worked for Daisy—why not for her?

It was so easy to get sucked in. Will was gorgeous. Will was charming. And even on a wet, rainy, cold night he made her feel like the most special person in the universe.

'Once we get through this, let's go someplace else. Let's go someplace it's just the two of us. I didn't want to share this with anyone else, Rose. And I don't want to share you either.' His lips were hovering just above her own. His warm breath heating her skin.

All she could see in this dim light was the dark blue rim around his eyes. The thing that she'd first noticed about him. The thing that had drawn her in and made her heart do that first little flip-flop.

There were no alarm bells ringing. No 'do this and you'll regret it' voices screaming in her head. Maybe, for the first time ever, she was really ready to take a chance on love?

His lips made contact with hers. It was the briefest of kisses. The warmest of kisses. Telling her everything she wanted to know and sending signals that her body was screaming for.

She couldn't walk away from Will right now if she tried.

So she stayed there, with Will's broad arms wrapped around her, sending a little heat into her numb bum and chilled bones. It felt right. It felt secure. It felt as if this was the place she was supposed to be.

Part of her brain kept ticking. She'd need to come clean with Violet. And Daisy. She'd need to tell her sisters how she really felt. All of this wasn't true until she'd done that. Her family were so important to her. But she would wait. She would wait until after the whole PR announcement tomorrow and the wedding renewal.

It would give her a little time—a little space to have confidence to trust her instincts once again.

Nothing would happen before that—surely?

CHAPTER ELEVEN

HER EYES FLICKERED OPEN. She could hear Will's breathing next to her, feel the rise and fall of his chest against her back. His arm was curled around her. Waking up next to Will this time was an entirely different sensation.

Her eyes wandered to the clock and widened in shock. It was nearly midday. Will had booked them into a boutique hotel in the West End of London. When they'd finished their night on the street she'd been utterly exhausted. The journalist had been waiting for Will and he'd done a short interview without letting go of her hand. Then he'd brought her to this hotel and done a whole lot more before they'd finally fallen asleep.

Her heart started thudding against her chest. There was a host of further interviews later today, then the TV show tonight with the reveal of the winning dare. She'd promised she'd be there. But right now she had to get home and do some work on her mother's bangle. Time was running out. She didn't just have commitments to Will to fulfil—she'd commitments to her family.

Especially now. Especially after what had just happened between them. She needed to talk to Violet sooner rather than later.

In a familiar motion she slipped out from under the covers. Her clothes were lying across the floor and she picked them up and slipped them back on. She should wake him. She really should. But he'd been every bit as exhausted as she'd been. She could let him sleep and order him breakfast in an hour or so. That way she'd have time to get across London and put in a few hours' work on the bangle before she had to get back for the TV show. If she woke him now he might try and distract her. And it was likely that she wouldn't say no.

She grabbed her phone. Out of charge and she'd forgotten to bring her charger—typical. She bent over the bed and laid a gentle kiss on his forehead. He didn't even flicker. Just kept breathing deeply. So she smiled and slipped out of the door, remembering exactly what had happened earlier that morning on her trip back across London.

Something wasn't right. The space in the bed next to him wasn't filled with a warm, comfortable body. There was just a little divot in the bed where that warm body should be.

Will's eyes flickered open, first to the space beside him, then to the bathroom door. Every part of his body was coiled up right now, hoping that any second there would be a flush, a sound of running water and Rose would walk out of the door. But everything was silent.

The knock at the door nearly gave him heart failure and sent him bolt upright in bed. The door opened with a member of the staff carrying a tray that he set next to the bed. 'Breakfast for you, Mr Carter.'

'I didn't order breakfast.' His stomach grumbled loudly as if it were part of the bad joke.

The staff member gave a nervous smile. 'The young lady ordered it for you.'

Will flung the cover back and went to stand up—right until he realised he wasn't wearing anything. The poor guy was already walking backwards to the door. He covered himself quickly. 'The young lady? Where is she?'

The guy couldn't get out of the room quickly enough. 'I think she left, sir,' he said as he pulled the door closed behind him. The smell of bacon, eggs and coffee filled the room as Will sagged back on the bed.

She'd left? Why on earth would she leave after the morning they'd had together? Will's stomach curled. Had he misread the signals? Had he misread Rose completely?

He grabbed his phone and dialled her number. Straight to voicemail. He sent a text. Delivered. He held the phone in his hand for a few minutes, willing her to reply. Nothing.

This couldn't be happening. Why on earth would Rose send him up breakfast but leave without saying goodbye—or, worse, without leaving a message? He looked around for pen and paper. But there was nothing obvious.

He pushed the breakfast tray away. He couldn't stomach anything right now. Not while everything he'd wished for was hanging in the air. His phone beeped and he jumped. But it wasn't a message. It was a reminder that the TV studio car would be picking him up in an hour. He wasn't on until six that night but they wanted to rehearse and since the whole show was about him and his charity he could hardly let them down.

Clothes. He needed new clothes. His fingers were still clenched around his phone, rapidly turning white. Rose would have to wait until later.

She was out of breath and cursing herself like mad.

'What's the name?' The guy at the front desk looked distinctly uninterested.

'Rose Huntingdon-Cross.'

He gave a cursory glance at the list and shook his head. 'Not on it.'

'What do you mean I'm not on it? I'm the one that arranged the interview.'

The guy almost sneered. 'You're not on the list.'

She could feel the pressure building in her chest and resisted the urge to grab the guy by the nape of the neck and drag him across the desk. She'd never use the 'Do you know who I am?' card but she hated ineptitude.

She folded her arms across her chest. 'I'm here for Paul Scholand's interview with Will Carter— you know, the Runaway Groom? I can give you the name of each and every one of his fiancées that must have checked in with you by now.'

The guy didn't even blink. 'Not on the list,' he said again. It was almost like a challenge.

She took a deep breath. 'Why don't you check under Cross? People often list my surname wrongly.'

His eyes went reluctantly to the page again and he blinked. 'Hmm. Cross by name, cross by nature?' he said in a sing-song voice. She really could pull him across the desk and thump him.

'You bet,' was her reply.

He gestured with his hand, waving her in, and she strode past without a second glance.

Once she was through she found the studio no problem. Paul Scholand had been interviewing out of the same studio for the last five years and Rose had been there on a number of occasions with the band—in fact, she was due back in another month.

But today was a bit different. The studio was normally always slick and smooth but with four extra women, who for reasons unknown to Rose seemed to be being kept apart, along with Will—who seemed to be being kept apart from *everyone*—the studio runners and assistants seemed harassed to death.

This thing had just taken root and sprouted into a complete forest. One she wasn't even sure she wanted to enter. She gulped. If this was how she was feeling—how on earth must Will be feeling?

She reached into her pocket. Nothing. Then remembered she hadn't even charged her phone from this morning. Darn it. Things had got a bit fraught when she was in her workshop. There had been problems with one of the kinds of gold. She was going to have to get more and it would take more than a day to arrive. All cutting into her time to work and make the bangle on time. It was her own fault. She'd been distracted when she'd started work and not totally focused on the job. Under normal circumstances she would have noticed a problem with the gold straight away. But no. She was too busy dreaming of the feel of Will's hands on her skin and his lips coming into contact with that sensitive area at the bottom of her neck.

Her hand automatically lifted to the area. Whenever she thought of him her skin tingled.

She looked around, trying to see him through the crowded studio. Her eyes locked on another set that was watching her carefully. Angie—one of Will's ex-fiancées.

Her feet hesitated for a second before she put a smile on her face and walked over, holding her hand out. 'Angie, it's so nice to meet you. Thank you for doing this. The phone lines are doing brilliantly. We're raising lots of money for the charity.'

Angie gave a controlled nod of her head. She was in the middle of getting her hair and make-up done. 'That's really good to know. I'm glad it's going well.'

Rose felt something creep up her spine. Angie was being very reserved. Had she done something to offend her?

'And thank you so much for putting me in touch with Deb. Her cakes are to die for. It was a real weight off my mind.'

As if on cue Angie pushed forward a plastic tub towards Rose. 'Deb sent something else for you to try. This is chocolate and hazelnut sponge. She wondered if you wanted some extra cupcakes for later?'

Rose picked up the tub straight away. She couldn't wait to try it. 'Oh, thank you, this is great. I'll give her a call later.'

Angie glanced sideways, as if to check to make sure no one else was listening. 'Be careful,' she said in a low voice. 'You've got that glow about you, Rose. Believe me, it can fade quickly. You're a nice girl.'

Rose opened her mouth to deny everything but the studio hairdresser had appeared again and was fussing around Angie. She walked away with her mouth hanging open. *Angie could tell just by looking at her?* How was that even possible? Nothing had happened until this morning. Up until then it had only been a few kisses. Nothing of any significance. And if she kept saying that she might actually believe it.

Will was at the other side of the studio with Paul Scholand. She lifted her hand to give him a wave and he wrinkled his brow, as if he was trying to work out who it was. She was forgetting. The studio lights were directly in his eyes.

She wandered closer. Round the back of the cameras and right round to the other side of the studio.

'You,' came the voice behind her. She spun on

her heels and pulled the plastic tub a little closer, as if it were some kind of shield. Melissa Kirkwood had that kind of effect on people. This was a woman that certainly hadn't got over the Runaway Groom. She was the one who'd suggested dunking Will in the Thames.

'What can I do for you, Melissa?' Rose tried her sweetest voice. She'd no intention of doing anything for Melissa; she already couldn't wait to get away from her.

Melissa folded her arms across her ample chest. She was wearing a bright pink dress with a slash right down the front. One of the studio hairdressers was behind her, teasing her hair into waves. Melissa had obviously decided there was no need to be as discreet as Angie.

'So are you floating on a cloud right now? Thinking that Will could never look at another woman the way he looks at you? Has he told you that he loves you yet?' she sneered. 'Because we've all been there, honey. Don't think you're special.'

It was like having someone tip a whole bucket of ice over your head.

What was it with these women? Did she have a neon sign above her head?

'I have no idea what you're talking about,' she said quickly.

'Sure, honey, that's what they all say before the

engagement ring appears, then your groom races down the aisle like he's being chased by killer zombies. It's written all over your face. You're just the next sucker in line.'

She could feel the colour rush up into her cheeks. Two ex-fiancées in almost the same number of minutes accusing her of the same thing. Was there a camera in the hotel room this morning? Last thing she wanted was to end up part of a sex-tape scandal like her sister.

She turned and walked away from Melissa. She'd already heard enough.

Will was standing at the edge of the set now while one of the make-up girls dusted some powder on his face. She was batting her eyelids and talking incessantly, but his gaze came into direct contact with Rose's.

It only took two strides to cross the space. 'Where did you go? I called you. Why didn't you call me back?'

Rose hesitated; her cheeks were still flushed from the comments from Angie and Melissa. She hated that people seemed to be able to read her so easily—particularly when she hadn't even had a chance to speak to her sisters. Was she really ready for this?

Her hesitation caused something to sweep over Will's face. He looked hurt. Even a little angry.

Paul Scholand was on his feet. 'Are you ready, Will? It's time for the countdown.'

Will nodded. 'Wait here,' he said quickly to her, shooting her a glance that made her insides curl up.

Everything about her felt in flux. She wanted to tell him the truth. She was confused. She needed time to think. She needed time to talk to her family. Last night and this morning had been great. She'd almost been convinced that he meant everything that he'd said.

But being here, in amongst the women he'd 'loved' before, was overwhelming. Words that he'd never said to her. She felt crowded—swamped. She felt as if there weren't enough room in the building for her own feelings while there was a huge rush of female hormones everywhere else. How on earth could she know how Will really felt about her here and now? This had disaster written all over it.

Will could feel the claustrophobia in the room. None of this was good. Paul kept looking at him reassuringly and patting him on the knee. He must sense that Will really just wanted to bolt from the studio.

The cameraman gave the signal and the theme tune started reverberating around the studio. On the other side of the studio, his four exes were being lined up on a curved sofa. He winced. Some of them had exchanged words in the past. He just hoped the studio had prepared for this adequately.

No matter how much he squinted at the spotlights he couldn't see Rose. All he'd felt from her was an overwhelming sense of panic. She'd left this morning as if she'd had second thoughts. She hadn't responded to any of his messages. And for the first time ever Will felt as if the shoe was on the other foot. He wanted Rose to feel the same as he did. He *needed* Rose to feel the same way he did.

Otherwise all his plans would be for nothing and he was about to make an even bigger fool of himself than normal.

Paul was talking now, playing the audience a clip showing each of his ex-fiancées talking about choosing their dare for him.

He looked at the four women. At one point he'd loved every one of them. At least he'd thought he had. He recognised it now as infatuation.

Nothing like what he felt for Rose. She was his first thought in the morning and his last thought at night. He'd seen her vulnerability last night. He'd wanted to do everything he could to protect the woman that he loved.

He wasn't running scared from Rose. Just the

opposite. He was running towards her so quickly he was afraid he'd scare her off.

What if he'd misjudged the situation completely and she really didn't want to take things that far? All he knew was it was so important to him to show her that she was different. That she was *The One*. To show her he wasn't the Runaway Groom any more.

Paul touched his arm. 'Are you ready for the final figure?'

Will blinked. He hadn't been paying the slightest bit of attention.

Paul was still smiling his perfect TV smile. 'Would you like to give the audience a little insight into why this charity is so important to you?'

Focus. Will nodded. This was the important bit. 'The charity is so important to me because I've had a friend affected by homelessness. There are a lot of misconceptions about people who live on the streets. Not all are drug addicts or alcoholics. Not all have been in trouble with the police. My friend hadn't done anything wrong, but because of the economic downturn his company went out of business. As a result he lost his home. He couldn't apply for jobs because he didn't have a permanent address. He didn't have family to turn to. He was embarrassed to tell his friends. I only found out after he was stabbed on the streets one night and the police contacted me because they found my card amongst his things. I want people to understand that there are a whole host of reasons people end up on the streets and there are lots of things we can do to help prevent it. Find out where your nearest shelter is. See what you can do to help. It doesn't have to be a lot. It can be donating clothes, donating food. It can be helping out in the kitchen. It can be helping people learn new skills.'

Paul nodded solemnly and turned to the camera. 'The votes have now closed. We're just about to find out how much money has been raised for charity. Ladies, are you ready?'

The camera panned along the four women with smiles on their faces. This was so not Will's idea of a good time. But if it got the message across he really didn't care.

'Is there any particular dare you'd like to avoid, Will?'

He shook his head. 'Paul, I'm willing to do whatever the public voted on no matter how humiliating it is. I just want to thank each and every person who picked up the phone and voted, contributing to the fund.' He put his hand on his chest. 'Thank you all from the bottom of my heart.'

Paul waited for the drum roll. It seemed to last for ever. Dramatic TV seemed to be his forte.

'Voting on the dares has finished. Will Carter, the total amount of money raised for your homeless charity is…one point one million pounds!'

Will's legs took on a life of their own and he shot upright with the wildest yell, punching the air. 'Yes!' His brain was jammed full of all the things the charity could do with the money. All the things that would make a difference for the people on the street. Staff. Housing. Employment. Rose was a genius. He could kiss her. He would kiss her.

Paul was still talking as Will pushed his way through the buzzing studio. He'd stopped listening to Paul. He'd stopped worrying about the cameras. All he wanted to do was find Rose.

Rose. There was a stunned smile on her face as he elbowed people out of the way to get to her. He picked her up in his arms and spun her around. 'Way to go, Rose! Have you any idea what this means?'

He didn't wait for an answer, just lowered her down and planted a kiss square on her lips, reaching his hands up to either side of her face. She tasted of strawberries. Sweet, juicy strawberries.

But she wasn't kissing back. Not as she usually did.

The buzz in the studio seemed to have died down a little. Will felt a tap on the shoulder. Paul, with a camera and light at his side. 'Will, who is this? Is this someone that we all should meet? Could this be your newest fiancée?'

He felt her bristle under his touch, every muscle in her body tensing. She pulled her lips away from his.

Panic. That was all he could see in her eyes. He'd misjudged this so badly. The one thing he didn't want to do. He'd just been swept away by the momentum of the event, and the memories of this morning. He hadn't even asked Rose if she was ready to go public and now, he'd just kissed her on national television in front of all his ex-fiancées. Could he get this any more wrong?

'Rose. Don't panic. This will be fine. Let me handle this,' he whispered.

But she looked horrified. Her hands fell from his sides. 'I'm not ready for this, Will.' Her words were cold. Definite.

Will stepped back as if stung. She looked hurt. She looked confused. *He'd* done this to her.

Will was used to women falling in love with him. He wasn't used to them stepping away. But Rose was different. And he'd known it from the start. It was why he loved her.

He turned to Paul. Right now, he could cheerfully punch him. Paul knew exactly who Rose was—he'd worked with her often enough.

'Rose is just a friend,' he said quickly before turning and beaming at the camera. 'I don't think

I'm quite ready for another fiancée, do you?' He gestured towards the four sitting women. 'Let's find out what dare I will be doing.'

Paul led him back over towards the TV sofas as his head spun round and round. How was he going to get this back? How was he going to sort this?

He glanced behind him. But the spot that Rose had been standing in was empty. She was gone.

Rose had never walked so quickly. Hot tears were spilling down her cheeks. *I don't think I'm quite ready for another fiancée, do you?*

How much more of a wake-up call did she need? Fiancées. He collected them like some kids collected dolls, or rubbers, or cars. Will Carter made promises he couldn't keep. He never saw things through to the main event.

That wasn't for her. It never would be. Rose was a traditionalist. She wanted what her mum and dad had. Love to last a lifetime. Nothing less would do. She wouldn't, *couldn't* settle for anything else.

She waited until she burst from the studio doors and the cool fresh air hit her before she finally released all the pent-up sobs. Home. She needed to go home. She needed to see her sisters.

Because at a time like this—only sisters would do.

CHAPTER TWELVE

WILL'S PHONE SOUNDED and he bolted across the room, knocking over a chair and leaping over his bed to reach it.

'Rose?' he answered breathlessly.

'Violet,' came the snarky reply. 'And I'm going to kill you with my bare hands, Will Carter.'

He sagged onto the bed. 'I thought it was Rose. I've left her a dozen messages and sent about a hundred texts.'

'I know. I've read them all. I'm in charge of Rose's phone now.'

He winced. The messages were private. They weren't really for family viewing.

'Please, just let me talk to her.'

'You did my sister, Will.' The blunt words cut through him. 'Of all the women in the world, you had to break my sister's heart.'

'No,' he cut in quickly. 'That's the last thing I want to do.'

'Well, it's too late.' He'd never heard Violet

like this. They'd been good friends for years with never a cross word.

'Violet, how long have you known me?'

There was a pause. 'Three years.'

'Have I ever lied to you?'

The pause stretched on and on. 'Well…no.'

'Violet, I love Rose with all my heart. I've even done something really crazy to prove it to her. But it's a bit hard to tell her about it if she won't even talk to me. I need your help.'

He could almost hear Violet's brain ticking over at the end of the phone. 'Violet, please. This is it for me. *Rose* is it for me. There won't ever be anyone else. Help me prove it to her.'

There was a loud sigh at the end of the phone. 'This better be good, Will.'

The relief was immense. 'It's better than good, Vi. I promise you. Here's what I need you to do…'

She hadn't had a minute. The last week had been frantic. Finalising every detail of her parents' wedding renewal. Trying to make sure that Daisy wasn't doing too much in her current condition and avoiding the messages from Will.

She'd had flowers every single day. Followed by balloons and cupcakes and the chocolates she'd loved at the wedding fair. It was nice. It was charming. But it was a token from a guy who was good at giving tokens, just not good at giving his whole heart.

Violet initially had been mad. Daisy had been sympathetic. But for the last few days both sisters had been surprisingly quiet. Maybe they were as caught up in the arrangements as she was.

But at last everything was ready—or at least it should be.

The marquees were finally in place and their corners filled with metallic heart-shaped balloons. The flower arches and covered chairs for the outside ceremony were complete. The weather had even decided to let the sun shine for the day.

People had been arriving at Huntingdon Hall since this morning. One celebrity friend after another with their little lists of demands. Rose had ignored every one of them. They were big enough to sort themselves out. She had her mother to deal with.

Daisy was lying across the chaise longue in her green gown, her hair in curls around her shoulders. 'Do you think I'm getting kankles?' she moaned.

'What on earth are kankles?' asked Violet. Her purple gown fitted perfectly and the beautiful exotic flowers that their mother had picked were the perfect explosion of colour against the rich jewel-toned gowns.

'Puffy ankles. Pregnant woman ankles. Do you think I'm getting them?'

Violet gave a cursory glance at Daisy's perfectly normal ankles in her flat jewelled sandals. 'Oh, belt up, Daisy.'

Rose winced. That was sharp—even for Violet, but she seemed a little on edge today.

'Well, girls, what do you think? Am I ready to face the world?'

Sherry Huntingdon looked magnificent. Her cream lace fishtail gown hugged every inch of her perfect body. All three girls were around her in an instant. Group hug. It was something they'd done since early childhood.

'You look spectacular, Mum,' said Rose quickly, trying to bat back the tears from her eyes. 'Dad won't be able to take his eyes off you.'

Daisy gave a little nod. 'Let's go to the staircase and get some pictures of that gown on the stairs. It will be gorgeous.' She was already thinking like the professional.

But Rose couldn't relax and be happy for the family portraits—even though she wanted to. Her stomach was wound like a tightly coiled spring. She should be able to relax. Everything was coming together. All the hours she'd spent working on the plans were finally coming to fruition. The endless nights she'd spent in her workshop working on the gold bangle for her mother would be worth it. She was sure of it. So why didn't she feel good?

Everything was perfect. Everything was hitch free. Three hundred people attended the wedding renewal ceremony. Amongst them, somewhere, would be Will—but she hadn't seen him yet.

After the renewal ceremony there were more photos, cake cutting, hors d'oeuvres and lots of wine. Then it was time for the sit-down meal.

Her father stood up to make a speech and she felt her breath hitch in her throat. He raised his glass. 'I want to thank you all for coming today, to see the wedding that my beautiful wife always deserved.' He gave a little laugh. 'Even if I am twenty-eight years too late. Most of you know that Sherry and I got married on a whim in Vegas. We hardly knew each other at all. But—' he raised his glass and looked at his wife '—when you know—you just know.' There was no hiding the love and devotion in his eyes. 'I want you all to know that every day that has been filled with Sherry has been perfect. We've fought. We've argued. There has been the odd occasion that we haven't spoken. But there hasn't been a single day I haven't wanted to be part of this partnership—part of this family with our three wonderful, if challenging, daughters.'

He picked up a box from the table. 'Lots of

people buy new wedding rings for a renewal ceremony. But Sherry and I didn't want to do that. We've had these rings for twenty-eight years and they've seen us through the good, the bad and the beautiful. They're sort of our lucky charms. So...' he gave a little nod to Rose '...with the help of one of our fabulously talented daughters, I got her something else.'

He handed over the box to Sherry, who opened it with shaking hands. She took out the bangle, the three twisted strands of gold intersected with a rose, a violet and a daisy. The recognition was instant and she leapt to her feet and wrapped her hands around Rick's neck. 'It couldn't be more perfect,' she declared.

The waiters were standing behind everyone, ready to put down the perfectly made first courses. But Rose's stomach was done. She couldn't even try a mouthful.

She'd always known it. It had played along in the background all along. This was what she wanted. This. The perfect part of knowing that every day, no matter what, there was one person you wanted by your side.

'Excuse me,' she said quickly to the person sitting next to her. 'I have to powder my nose.'

Her footsteps covered the gardens quickly, taking her back to the sanctity of the house. The quiet of the house, the coolness of the house.

She took a deep breath, closed her eyes and leaned against the cool wall. Hold it together. Stop being so pathetic. This is your parents' wedding renewal. All you need to do is get through the day. This isn't about you. This isn't about Will. This is about them.

The voices circulated in her head, but they did nothing to stop the tears pooling behind her eyelids. There was a small thud beside her, the sound of another pair of shoulders hitting the wall right next to her. Violet. Then a hand slid into hers. A broad, thick hand, its fingers interlocking with her own. Not Violet.

Her eyes flew open. 'Will.' She didn't want him to see her like this. She wanted him to see her when she was sure of herself, when she knew exactly how to react around him.

He let go of her hand and stepped in front of her, placing one hand above each shoulder, fencing her against the wall.

'Rose,' he said matter-of-factly. 'No phones, no messages.' He gave a wry smile. 'No flowers, no balloons, no cupcakes. Just you. And me.'

Her breath was caught somewhere in her throat. Halfway up and halfway down and not being of any use at all.

'I… I…' She couldn't find any suitable words.

He shook his head. 'Not I. Not you. Not me. Us. We need to talk about us, Rose.'

'There is no us.' The words rushed out.

'But there should be.' His reply was equally quick.

Her brain was working on overdrive. She had so many things she wanted to say. 'I'm sorry. I couldn't handle that day at the studio. When I saw all your exes lined up and looking at me I just felt as if I were the next lamb to the slaughter.'

He blinked. It wasn't her best choice of words. But her brain wasn't treading carefully right now.

'It was too much, Will. It was too soon. After what we'd just done and then Angie said something, then Melissa…and then you kissed me and Paul cracked that joke.'

He lifted a finger to her lips. 'Stop, Rose. Just stop.'

She stopped babbling and tried to think straight. He lifted his finger gently from her lips and placed it over his heart.

'Angie, Melissa, Paul.' He shook his head. 'You are the person that matters to me, Rose. All those women were my past. None of them matter. You're what matters, Rose. You are my future.'

She opened her mouth again and he shook his head to silence her. 'I should have known how you would feel in the studio. I didn't want to be there—why on earth would you? It was claustrophobic. They hadn't spent the night we just had. They hadn't seen what we'd just seen, or shared what we'd just shared. When Paul told me how much money we'd raised the first person I wanted to see, the first person I wanted to share that with, was you, Rose. Nobody else. You were the person I wanted to celebrate with.'

He raised his eyebrows and his mouth quirked. 'And I want to thank you for not coming to that department store and helping me sell women's lingerie all day dressed in nothing but a thong.'

She couldn't help but smile. The pictures of Will's butt had probably sold a million newspapers. The store had never had such good sales and had pledged part of them to the homeless charity.

She sighed. 'I just couldn't, Will. I needed some time. I needed some space.'

He reached up and wound his finger through one of her blonde curls. 'I get that. I do. But I've missed you. I've missed you every single day, Rose. I don't want to spend a single day without you.'

The lump in her throat was growing by the second. He was good. He was really good. And he was being sincere. But she still had the horrible doubts that she wasn't the only woman to hear those words and it was breaking her heart.

He touched her cheek. 'I love you, Rose. I don't want to be without you. I don't want to be without you ever.'

A tear slid down her cheek. She should be singing with joy and while part of her wanted to, she couldn't face the heartache that being left at the altar might bring. Not when she loved him with her whole heart.

It was just the two of them in the corridor. She had a clear, unblinking view of the dark rim around his eyes. Something she could spend the rest of her life looking at.

'And I can prove it.' He reached inside his jacket and her heart lurched.

No. Not this. Anything but this.

'I don't want to be your next fiancée,' she cried. The words just blurted out.

'And I don't want you to be my next fiancée,' he replied coolly. His hand came out slowly from his jacket pocket. It wasn't a ring box. It wasn't anything remotely like jewellery he was holding. It was a piece of paper. No matter what she'd said before, her heart gave a little sag.

He handed it to her silently and took his other hand down from the wall next to her head.

Her hands were trembling as she unfolded the paper. She stared at it for a few seconds. Blinking at the words. She couldn't make sense of it at all because she'd never seen anything like this before.

'What is it?' Her voice was shaking.

'It's our wedding banns. For tonight, for a wedding in the church on the island. I don't want you to be my fiancée, Rose. I want you to be my wife. I didn't know how else to prove it to you.'

'But…but…how did you do this?' Her hands were still trembling as she looked at the date. Sixteen days before. Now she really couldn't breathe. Her legs felt like jelly beneath her. 'You knew then?'

He nodded. 'I knew then, Rose. I didn't doubt it. The only person I had to convince was you.'

'You want us to get married today?'

He smiled and knelt down. 'This is how I'm supposed to do it, isn't it? I guess I just was scared you wouldn't let me get this far.'

He reached up and took both her hands. 'Rose Huntingdon-Cross. I love you with my whole heart and I want you to be the person I wake up next to every morning. And I don't care what continent we do that on. If you want to go back to New York and work, I'll come with you. If you want to keep designing wedding jewellery—I'll build you a whole workshop. Whatever you want, Rose, I'll do it.'

He bent forward and kissed the tips of her fingers, one after the other. 'I've listened to every single thing you've told me. You don't want a big wedding. Check. You loved the church on the island. Check. You don't want a runaway groom. Check. You want things to be simple. Check.

All you want is a dress, flowers and I've taken a gamble on a string of fairy lights. Check. You want someone who loves you with their whole heart. Check. You want the kind of love that your parents have—' he winked at her '—Violet let me in on that secret. Check. So, will you do me the honour of becoming my wife tonight? I love you, Rose. I'll never love anyone like you, and I'm hoping you feel the same way. Because I want that kind of love too, Rose. The kind that your parents have—the kind that lasts for ever.'

She couldn't believe it. She couldn't believe her ears. 'You really want to do this now—tonight? You planned this two weeks ago?'

'I planned this two weeks ago.'

'But how could you possibly have known?' She couldn't wipe the smile from her face.

He tilted his head. 'Because when you know, Rose, you just know. Remind you of anyone we know?'

The words flooded over her. He'd used her father's expression and it had never seemed so apt. It was time. It was time to let go and trust her instincts. She'd grown more than she could ever have predicted in the last three years. It was time to throw off the seeds of doubt. Will was standing in front of her declaring his love. He'd done all this for *her*. He'd done all this because he loved *her*. And she loved him with her whole heart.

She smiled. In her head she could see them already. Sitting on a little wooden bench with grey hair growing old together—of that, she had no doubt.

He stood up and put his hands on her hips. 'Ready to visit our island?'

She grinned. 'Our island. I like the sound of that...'

CHAPTER THIRTEEN

WHEN HER STOMACH flipped over now it was with pure excitement. They pulled up straight next to where the boat was moored. Even from here she could see multicoloured fairy lights strung across the thick trees on the island.

'What about witnesses?' It was the first time she'd given it any thought. The drive here had just been a blur.

Will touched her face. 'I spoke to Violet. If we'd tried to sneak your sisters away from the renewal it might have attracted some attention. They'll be waiting for us when we get back. Our witnesses—as long as you're happy—will be Judy and my friend, Arral. I invited him along specially.' She smiled and nodded as tears pooled in her eyes. He'd thought of everything.

She fingered the fine material of her blue dress. It wasn't quite what she'd imagined herself getting married in, but then again, this was how she'd always wanted to do it—just as her parents had—no fuss, just two people who loved each other saying their vows.

The journey to the island was smooth as silk. He helped her out of the boat at the other side and pointed her towards the cottage. 'There's a surprise for you in there. I'll give you a few minutes.'

She nodded as she walked into the cottage. It was just as beautiful as she remembered. But the ambience had changed. Last time it had been full of pent-up emotion and surging hormones. This time it was balanced. This time it was full of hope, promise and love.

She caught her breath. A full-length dress was hanging part way from the ceiling, just within her reach. It was a real-life wedding dress. Cream embroidery at the top with an embroidered tulle straight skirt, it was exactly what she would have picked for herself.

It only took a few minutes to slip out of the blue dress and into the cream one. On a table at the side were a few lemon roses tied with lemon and cream ribbons. All the while she'd thought Will was helping her plan her parents' renewal he'd actually been planning their own wedding.

There was a knock at the door. 'Rose? Is everything okay? Are you ready?' He sounded a little nervous.

She walked over and opened the door. He'd

changed into a grey suit with a matching lemon rose buttonhole. Her husband-to-be couldn't have looked more perfect.

She slid her hand into his. 'I can't wait.'

They walked hand in hand to the church. Will smiled as he opened the door and a wave of heart-shaped foil balloons burst from the doors and floated into the sky above. Then he led her down the aisle where their witnesses and celebrant stood waiting.

It was perfect. It was magical. The room was lit with fairy lights and candles. The evening light behind the stained-glass windows sent beautiful shards of rainbow reflections over the white walls.

She walked over and gave both Judy and Arral a kiss on the cheek. 'Thank you for coming,' she whispered. 'Thank you for sharing this with me and Will.'

The celebrant nodded. 'Can we begin?'

Rose took a deep breath and nodded, looking into the eyes of the man she loved. No Runaway Groom. No waiting. Will was about to become her husband.

They repeated their names and made their declarations. For a second Rose expected the church to be invaded by a wave of angry objecting ex-fiancées, but everything was silent.

Will turned to face his bride, holding up a plain

yellow band. 'This was the one thing I couldn't plan. I could hardly ask my wife to make her own wedding band without letting her in on the secret. So, I decided we'd make do for now because she'll have the rest of her life to change them if she wishes.'

Rose nodded. 'These will be perfect.'

Will held the ring poised at her finger. 'Rose Huntingdon-Cross. I love you more than I ever thought possible. I've shared things with you that I could never share with another living soul. You complete me. You are my world. I want to spend the rest of my life getting to know you more and promise to love you more each day until the end of my life.' He smiled at her. 'Because when you know—you just know.'

She let out a nervous laugh and picked up his wedding ring, her fingers trembling as she slid it onto his finger. 'Will Carter, you burst into my life in the most unpredictable way and will probably bear the scar for the rest of our lives. I love you, Will Carter, even though I was afraid to. You've taught me that after three years it's okay to trust my instincts again. You've taught me that people aren't always what we presume they are. You've taught me that there's a whole world out there that I knew nothing about. I want to spend the rest of my life working side by side with my husband and helping those who want to be helped. I want to grow with you, Will. I want to love you more each day. And you'll never be my runaway groom, you'll always be my husband, the man who has captured my heart.'

She leaned forward and they kissed. His hands sliding down her back and cupping her backside, pressing her against him. She wound her hands around his neck. She couldn't have planned anything more perfect. This was all she'd ever wanted from a wedding. Her and her husband saying their vows at a beautiful setting. Two people who loved each other for ever.

'Do we get to have our honeymoon in the cottage?' she whispered.

He shook his head. 'Oh, no. The honeymoon is a complete surprise. We'll be gone for three weeks.'

She pulled back. 'Three weeks? But what about the tour and the charity concert?' She put her hand to her mouth. 'Oh, no. I'm supposed to pick up that reporter from the airport in a few hours.'

Will laughed and shook his head. 'Oh, no, you don't. That's all under control. For the next three weeks Violet is in charge. I've given her your black planner and she's picking up Tom Buckley at the airport. She's even packed your case. All we need to do is go back and tell your parents and Daisy that we're married.'

'Really?' He'd thought of everything.

He held out his hand towards her and she slid her fingers into her husband's. 'Really.'

By the time they arrived back her father had just finished rocking out on the stage with his band. His hair was damp with sweat and his jacket and tie had been flung aside.

Daisy and Violet were pacing. It was obvious Violet hadn't been able to keep things to herself.

She rushed over straight away. There was no mistaking the look on her face; she was genuinely delighted. She grabbed hold of Rose's left hand. 'Have you done it? Are you genuinely Mrs Carter?'

Rose gave the tiniest nod; she couldn't hide the grin that spread from one ear to the other as she looked at her brand-new husband. 'Mrs Carter, wow.' She hadn't actually said the words out loud and they seemed unreal.

But that didn't stop Violet. 'Wheeeeee!' She let out a yell and jumped on Will, sending him flat out onto the grass. 'Finally!'

Will couldn't stop laughing. 'I take it you approve.'

Violet bent forward and kissed him on the forehead. 'Finally, I stop having to pretend to like all your fiancées.' She winked at Rose. 'This one, I love!'

'Rose!' Her mother's voice cut through the crowd of people.

Will stood up from the grass, dusted himself off and slid his hand into hers.

Sherry was gorgeous as ever. Her eyes widened slightly as she noticed the change in Rose's dress. She wrapped her arms around her daughter's shoulder. 'You look beautiful, darling.'

She reached her hand over to touch Will's cheek. 'I take it you have something to tell me, Mr Carter?'

Rick appeared at Sherry's side, sliding his arm around her waist. Rose was holding her breath, well aware that both her sisters were doing the same thing. But Rick Cross grinned and held out his hand towards Will. 'I take it she said yes?'

Will shook his hand. 'You've no idea the relief I felt.'

Sherry's eyebrows rose. 'You knew?'

Rick laughed. 'Of course I knew. Will's a traditionalist. He asked me a few weeks ago.'

Sherry shook her head. 'And you kept it a secret from me?'

Rick rolled his eyes. 'You and secrets, Sherry? Oh, no. I wasn't getting myself in that much trouble.'

'I've got something to tell you, too, Dad.' Rose's heart was thudding in her chest. She'd never been so sure of anything.

'What is it, honey?'

She intertwined her fingers with Will's. 'When I come back from my honeymoon I'll help with the final plans for the tour and then I'll be re-signing.' She shot Will a smile. 'I'm going to be working on my jewellery collection full-time.'

Her father gave a little nod of his head. It was almost as if he'd been expecting it.

He leaned over and kissed Rose's cheek. 'I take it you got the wedding you always wanted, beautiful?'

She breathed in deeply. Her parents were happy for her. Her sisters were happy for her.

And she had a husband she loved and trusted with her whole heart.

She leaned up and whispered in his ear. 'Can the honeymoon start now?'

Will slid his hands around her waist as his blue eyes twinkled. 'Absolutely.'

* * * * *

COMING NEXT MONTH FROM

HARLEQUIN®
Romance

Available June 2, 2015

#4475 HIS UNEXPECTED BABY BOMBSHELL
by Soraya Lane

Best friends Rebecca and Ben were the couple most likely to marry, but when their chemistry finally bubbled over, it was on the night Ben left to become an international polo player. Now he's back, and Rebecca must tell Ben he's a father!

#4476 FALLING FOR THE BRIDESMAID
Summer Weddings • by Sophie Pembroke

Violet Huntingdon-Cross is always the bridesmaid, but could journalist Tom be the one she's been waiting for? As Tom helps her discover that love isn't just something that happens to other people, will falling for each other lead them down the aisle?

#4477 A MILLIONAIRE FOR CINDERELLA
In Love with the Boss • by Barbara Wallace

Patience Rush doesn't need a knight in shining armor. She's perfectly happy working as a housekeeper...until Stuart Duchenko arrives. He knows she's hiding something, but what? As they grow closer, Patience realizes that letting go of her past is the only way to a blissful future with Stuart...

#4478 FROM PARADISE...TO PREGNANT!
by Kandy Shepherd

A week in Bali was Zoe's dream vacation—until the island is hit by an earthquake! Trapped alongside high school crush Mitch, they seek comfort in each other's arms... But Zoe soon discovers she's pregnant! Can one night lead to parenthood *and* a lifetime of love?

HRLPCNM0515

LARGER-PRINT BOOKS!

GET 2 FREE LARGER-PRINT NOVELS PLUS
2 FREE GIFTS!

HARLEQUIN®

Romance

From the Heart, For the Heart

YES! Please send me 2 FREE LARGER-PRINT Harlequin® Romance novels and my 2 FREE gifts (gifts are worth about $10). After receiving them, if I don't wish to receive any more books, I can return the shipping statement marked "cancel." If I don't cancel, I will receive 4 brand-new novels every month and be billed just $5.09 per book in the U.S. or $5.49 per book in Canada. That's a savings of at least 15% off the cover price! It's quite a bargain! Shipping and handling is just 50¢ per book in the U.S. and 75¢ per book in Canada.* I understand that accepting the 2 free books and gifts places me under no obligation to buy anything. I can always return a shipment and cancel at any time. Even if I never buy another book, the two free books and gifts are mine to keep forever.

119/319 HDN GHWC

Name	(PLEASE PRINT)	
Address		Apt. #
City	State/Prov.	Zip/Postal Code

Signature (if under 18, a parent or guardian must sign)

Mail to the **Reader Service**:
IN U.S.A.: P.O. Box 1867, Buffalo, NY 14240-1867
IN CANADA: P.O. Box 609, Fort Erie, Ontario L2A 5X3
Want to try two free books from another line?
Call 1-800-873-8635 or visit www.ReaderService.com.

She stopped, close enough that she could almost feel his breath on her face, but still not touching. Violet looked up into his eyes and saw the control there. He was holding back. So she wouldn't.

Bringing one hand up to rest against his chest, she felt the thump of his heart through his shirt and knew she wanted to be close to that beat for as long as he'd let her. Slowly, she rose up onto her tiptoes, enjoying the fact that he was tall enough that she needed to. And then, without breaking eye contact for a moment, Violet kissed him.

It only took a moment before he responded, and Violet let herself relax into the kiss as his arms came up to hold her close. The celebrity wedding melted away, and all she knew was the feel of his body against hers and the taste of him on her lips. This. This was what she needed. Why had she denied herself this for so long?

And how could it be that kissing Tom somehow tasted like trust?

Eventually, though, she had to pull away. Tom's arms

kept her pressed against him, even as she dropped down to her normal height, looking up into his moss-green eyes.

"Is this where I give you some kind of line about getting to know me even better?" Tom asked, one eyebrow raised.

Violet's laugh bubbled up inside her, as if kissing Tom had released all the joy she'd kept buried deep down. "I think it probably is, yes."

"In that case, how long do you think we need to stay at this party?"

"There's five hundred people here," Violet pointed out. "What are the chances of them missing just two?"

"Good point." And with a warm smile spreading across his face, Tom grabbed Violet's hand and they ran for the waiting car.

Don't miss this enchanting conclusion to the
SUMMER WEDDINGS *trilogy,*
FALLING FOR THE BRIDESMAID.
Available June 2015 wherever
Harlequin® Romance books and ebooks are sold.

www.Harlequin.com

HREXP0515